Frank and Ruby, Canada

CHANCE DEVELOPMENTS

Chance Developments

Alexander McCall Smith

PANTHEON BOOKS NEW YORK

This is a work of fiction. Names, characters, places, and incidents either are the product of the author's imagination or are used fictitiously. Any resemblance to actual persons, living or dead, events, or locales is entirely coincidental.

 Published in the United States by Pantheon Books, a division of Penguin Random House LLC, New York, and in Canada by Alfred A. Knopf Canada, a division of Penguin Random House Canada Limited, Toronto. Originally published in hardcover in Great Britain by Polygon Books, an imprint of Birlinn Limited, Edinburgh, in 2015.

Pantheon Books and colophon are registered trademarks of Penguin Random House LLC.

Grateful acknowledgment is made to Historic Environment Scotland for permission to reprint the photographs on pages 3 (#SC 679143; Tom and Sybil Gray Collection), 51 (#DP 102639), 109 (#PD 102508), 159 (#DP 096394), and 193 (#DP 097355).

Library of Congress Cataloging-in-Publication Data
McCall Smith, Alexander, [date] author.
Title: Chance developments : stories / Alexander McCall Smith.
LCCN 2015042318. ISBN 9781101871256 (hardcover). ISBN 9781101871263 (ebook).
BISAC: FICTION/Contemporary Women. FICTION/Humorous. FICTION/Short Stories (single author).
LCC PR6063.C326 A6 2016 DDC 823/.914—dc23
LC record available at: lccn.loc.gov/2015042318

www.pantheonbooks.com

Cover image © Historic Environment Scotland
Jacket design by Oliver Munday

Printed in the United States of America
First American Edition
9 8 7 6 5 4 3 2 1

This book is for Nicholas and Liz Ellenbogen

CONTENTS

AUTHOR'S NOTE

SOME YEARS AGO I WAS INVITED BY THE DISTINGUISHED American museum curator Robert Flynn Johnson to write an introduction to a book he was about to publish. This book was a collection of "orphaned" photographs—old black-and-white photographs that had no clear provenance and featured unknown people in all sorts of situations. In that introduction I chose to create stories around some of these photographs—very short stories in that case, and most of them highly unlikely. I enjoyed the experience so much that I decided that one day I would do an entire book of photographically inspired stories.

Recently I wrote a book about Edinburgh based on the magnificent collection of photographs owned by the conservation body Historic Environment Scotland. I asked my editor for that book, Jamie Crawford, if he might find me a selection of black-and-white photographs of people from the past so that I could imagine the stories behind the images. He came up with an intriguing collection, and the result is this offering. We know nothing about the real people in these photographs—by the age of the prints none of them will still be alive; these stories imagine who they might have been and what their personal history was. The people in the stories, then, are not the same as the people in the photographs: rather, they are suggested by them. They are all love stories in one sense or another, because love lies at the heart of our experience of the world. They are also about friendship, love's cognate, and frequently both its prequel and sequel.

Love transforms the people in these stories, as it may transform any of us. In some cases it will not be reciprocated as fully as it might be, but if that happens we could do worse than to remember the advice of the poet W. H. Auden, who tells us that "If equal affection cannot be, then let the more loving one be me." I have always thought that those lines can be read in such a way as somehow to express an entire philosophy of life, a guide to all of us on our journey.

Alexander McCall Smith

CHANCE DEVELOPMENTS

Sister Flora's First Day of Freedom

1

They did their best to be generous to Sister Flora when she left the convent, but the dresses they gave her left something to be desired. A great deal, in fact, according to some.

"Well!" muttered one of the laywomen who helped with the vegetable garden. "Did you see the outfits they gave her? You wouldn't think it was 1961—more like 1931!"

She was right about the dresses, of which there were two. Both had been donated to the convent by the women's guild at the local church, and both were irretrievably dull. One was made of beige bombazine, the other of a rough wool fabric of the sort that a rural schoolmistress might have worn decades earlier. Both had been retrieved from somebody's wardrobe, both had a faint odour of camphor, although neither appeared to have suffered any moth damage.

They also gave her an unbecoming grey cardigan, a plain, full-length coat, and a pair of shoes that was slightly too small. The shoes, at least, were new, although they, too, were far from fashionable. Then there was a small suitcase, a sponge bag of toiletries, and an envelope containing fifteen pounds.

"We might have entertained the possibility of giving you a slightly larger sum," said the Mother Superior, "but since you are going to be living with your aunt you will have no rent to pay, and I imagine your aunt, being the pious woman she is, will provide necessities."

Flora smiled. "I don't really deserve anything," she said. "I brought nothing with me when I came ten years ago, and I don't think I should leave with anything."

"That's a very good attitude," the Mother Superior continued. "Mind you, I gather that money is not going to be a problem. This sum is purely to tide you over until such time as your . . . your arrangements are in place."

"I have been most fortunate," she said. "I am not intending to forget that, Mother."

"No," said the Mother Superior. "I don't imagine you will. You always had a very good disposition, you know. I'm sorry that one or two people have been passing . . . well, what can only be described as uncharitable remarks." She looked away, her lips pursed in disapproval. "I heard somebody say they thought that money had interfered with God's plan for you."

"I don't think that's entirely fair," said Flora.

"Neither do I," said the Mother Superior. "And indeed I imagine there are circumstances that suggest that God's plan for certain people is that they *should* have money. After all, if nobody had any money, then who would give to the Holy Church?"

"Precisely," said Flora.

The Mother Superior looked out of the window. "I was very reassured to hear that you hadn't lost your faith. That was a great comfort to me, you know."

"I haven't lost it," said Flora. "It's just that . . . oh, I suppose it's just that I decided that I'm not cut out for the religious life. I've enjoyed it well enough, but I feel that somehow life is passing me by."

"Quite understandable, my child," said the Mother Superior.

"And I thought that I really had to make a decision one way or the other. So I decided that I would go out into the world. It just seemed the right thing for me to do."

"We all understand," said the Mother Superior. "I understand; poor Sister Frances understands—just; and Father Sullivan understands. You'll be happy doing God's work in the wider world—whatever that happens to be."

"I hope so."

"And, of course," continued the Mother Superior, "you will be a wealthy woman."

Sister Flora lowered her eyes. "I didn't reach the decision because of that," she said. "I had already decided."

"Oh, I know that," said the Mother Superior. "I wasn't for a moment suggesting *post hoc, propter hoc*. But being wealthy will be . . . well, rather *nice*, don't you think?"

2

It was difficult for her to remember when it dawned on her that she had a vocation. Some people spoke of a moment of revelation—a moment of certainty—the meaning of which was completely clear. One of the younger sisters had said that it had come to her one morning when she got out of bed and opened the window. "There was a particular sort of light," she said. "It filled the sky, and I knew at once that I was being called." Another said that it had come to her in a dream, when she had seen the Virgin herself, who had beckoned her. That, she said, was a sign that would only come once in a lifetime and should not be taken lightly, nor questioned.

It had been different for Flora. She had never had a sense of controlling her own future, of making decisions about what she would do—this, it seemed to her, had been done for her by others. It was not that anybody imposed their will on her; it was more gentle than that. There were suggestions that she had been thinking of a religious life all along; that it was something for which she had somehow shown an aptitude. And then, just as she was about to leave school, there had been that fateful conversation with Sister Angela, a particularly sympathetic nun, who had said, "There will always be a place for you in the Order, you know." And she had been flattered that she should be thought of in this way.

At university she had become involved in the Catholic chaplaincy, and again assumptions were made. "It's easy for you," one of her friends had said. "You're obviously going to end up in the Church. You don't have to look for something."

Flora had simply said, "No, I suppose I don't." And that, she thought, was the moment at which the decision—if one could call it that—was made. She finished her degree, and took a year's teaching diploma after that before entering the convent as a novice. They were delighted that she had joined them; they ran a school and there was a shortage of nuns with recent, recognised teaching qualifications. A newly minted graduate of the University of Glasgow—in mathematics, of all things—was exactly the sort of young woman the convent wanted.

Her parents were proud of her. They were now elderly, and she was their only child. Any thoughts they had about losing the daughter who might care for them in their old age were eclipsed by their pleasure in having provided the Church, which was at the core of their lives, with such a charming servant.

Her father died a month after she took her final vows, and her mother survived him by barely a year. Thereafter her only family was her aunt and uncle, a childless couple, who lived in a small town on the Clyde estuary. This uncle had been a successful hotelier and caterer, who had made wise investments in land on the outskirts of the city. Flora was aware that he was well off, but it had never occurred to her that he would direct that a large part of his estate was to go to her. She had met the lawyer at his funeral, a thin man with a nasal voice, who had been introduced to her by her aunt at the funeral tea.

"I was always a great admirer of your uncle," said the lawyer. "His good works were legion, you know."

She smiled. "He will be missed," she said.

The lawyer adjusted his tie. "I will need to speak to you at some point," he said. "Not here, of course—this isn't really the moment. But you are, you may know, his heir."

She looked at him blankly. "But my aunt?"

"She is very well provided for already," said the lawyer. "You're what we call the residuary beneficiary, and that will involve a substantial amount. A very substantial amount."

She was not sure what to say. "Well . . ."

"These provisions were made when you were still at university," he said. "He did not change them after you went into the convent."

"Oh."

"They're perfectly valid, of course. I don't anticipate any problem. But you might care to be advised on what to do . . ." He made a gesture that she found hard to interpret—a rolling of the hand. Was this because he had never had to deal with a legacy to somebody who had taken a vow of poverty?

"Will it be possible for me to come to see you at the convent?" he asked.

She nodded. "If you telephone."

He looked apologetic. "I wasn't sure whether it was one of those open orders."

"We are. We're not enclosed."

He looked relieved. "I had an aunt in Dublin," he said. "She was a nun and none of the family ever saw her."

"There are some orders that keep themselves away from the world. It's to do with prayer." She paused. "Telephone the school office. The secretary there is Mrs. Morrison. She'll make an appointment. It's best just after school's out—about four."

He reached out to take her hand briefly. "I'll do that, and I'm so sorry about your uncle. There are so few good people these days that the loss of one of them makes such a difference."

She thanked him, and he moved away. She closed her eyes. She wondered whether she had brought this upon herself; that this was somehow a consequence of having taken the decision to leave the convent. She knew it was irrational, but she had struggled for years with guilt and a tendency to give in to superstition. She had bargained with herself, identifying what she had to do to avert disaster: one more rosary, just one, or something dreadful will happen; one further novena or something would happen to one of the girls in her class—these were the little pacts, familiar to anybody who suffers from obsessive-compulsive disorder; these were the ways in which she negotiated her way through life.

The lawyer came to see her two weeks later. He brought her aunt, and the three of them sat facing one another in the convent parlour. The floor was highly polished—that was the mark, she thought, of a nun's parlour anywhere in the world: the smell of polish, the air of scrupulous, antiseptic tidiness.

The Mother Superior had suggested that she might be there too. "I'd be perfectly happy to see Mr. O'Malley with you," she said. "His brother is in the St. Vincent de Paul Society and I've met him. That family had a daughter here some years back—I think she was his niece."

"That's very kind of you, Mother, but I think my aunt might prefer the meeting to be a small one."

"If that's what she wants . . ."

"Yes, it is. Thank you all the same."

Now they sat together in the rather faded and uncomfortable Morris chairs, each with a cup of tea on the small occasional table beside them.

The lawyer produced a file and extracted several copies of a document.

"Mr. O'Malley wanted to explain things to you," said her aunt. "He's always been very good at translating legal documents into plain English."

The lawyer smiled weakly. "I do my best," he said. "And your uncle's will is far from complicated. May I tell you—in the most general terms, of course—what he had in mind?"

"He was always very well organised," said the aunt. "He never liked disorder."

"Admirable," said the lawyer.

She was given a copy of the document. She glanced at it and saw her uncle's signature. It saddened her; she had loved him. He was a kind man.

"Effectively, what he asked his executors to do is to create two trusts," said the lawyer. "One is an offshoot of an existing trust he had created for your aunt, and this makes provision for her maintenance at, well, I hope she will agree, a very comfortable level."

"Very," said the aunt.

"There are certain legacies," the lawyer continued. "There is something for the St. Vincent de Paul Society and there is an outstandingly generous one to the Diocese of Glasgow. After that, everything goes into your fund, to be administered by trustees appointed under the will."

"There's an awful lot in that," said the aunt. "All the property in Renfrew. His shareholdings in ICI. The Clydesdale Bank funds. It's a lot of money, Flora."

"The trustees have the power to make disbursements," said the lawyer. "That means they will meet such reasonable requests as you may make. Funds should be adequate for . . . well, for just about everything you would care to do with it."

He looked at her expectantly and she, in her turn, glanced at her aunt. The aunt smiled encouragingly.

"I have decided to leave the Order," said Flora.

The aunt's surprise was evident. "Well," she said. "That *is* news."

The lawyer frowned. "I must say that I have always said to legatees that they should sleep on any decisions they make. Sometimes the prospect of an infusion of funds makes people behave a bit rashly. Not that this would apply to you, of course, but I should perhaps sound a note of caution."

Flora shook her head. "I've been thinking about this for some time." She turned to the aunt. "I was going to tell you, but then Uncle Hector became ill and I never got round to it."

The aunt reassured her. "Of course, my dear. And I must say that I'm rather relieved. I know it's an important calling, but I've always felt it a pity that you hadn't led a life before you went in. I've always thought you left the world before you got to know it."

"Well, I'm going to do something about that now. I'm thirty-two, so I don't think it's too late."

"Not in the least," said the lawyer. "We shall hold funds for you in our clients' account," he added. "They will be available when and as you need them."

"Where are you going to go?" asked the aunt.

She shrugged.

"Come to me," said the aunt. "Stay as long as you like."

"You could easily afford a flat or house of your own," said the lawyer. "It's exactly the sort of purchase that trustees are very happy to authorise."

"I'll think about it," said Flora.

That ended the business side of the conversation, and as they chatted over a cup of tea, she thought, *Would it be better to get a flat before a husband, or get a husband first and then a flat?* She would have like to have asked them, but she could not, because neither knew the nature of her plans just yet, and she was eager not to play her hand too soon.

3

She might have continued as a teacher; she might have continued as a nun, if it had been possible to live with a less doctrinaire faith with conviction. But she could not see how that would work. As a nun she felt she had to adhere to the Church more strictly than a layperson, and she felt that doing this would be hypocritical on her part. So she would take a sabbatical from the Church. She might still go to Mass, but she would give even that a break for a while. She would explore other avenues. She would look at things critically. She would find God in places she had been afraid to look. And she would do all this without Father Sullivan or the bishop telling her what she could think and do. They are fine men, but I am my own person, she thought, I am entitled to look for God in this world in the way *I* choose to do . . . She paused. Goodness! I'm becoming a Protestant—or almost; she, from a family steeped in Catholicism, whose social life, whose very sense of identity was rooted in a tight, exclusive Catholic world—she was becoming, of all things, a Protestant.

And why should she not take just a look at Protestantism and what it had to offer? She would not do anything immediately, but she would do it. It would shock her aunt and the few cousins she had on her mother's side, for whom loyalty to Catholicism was a tribal matter and for whom the bonds that secured them to their religion were as hoops of steel. But it was her life she was thinking about, and she should be able to do with it what *she* wanted to do.

"The dear sisters," said the aunt, "have no clothes sense, do they, bless them."

She was surveying the beige bombazine with a bemused expression.

"It's actually a rather fine fabric," said Flora, fingering the sleeve of the dress. "But it looks so old-fashioned, doesn't it?"

"I'm afraid it does," agreed the aunt. "You can go shopping tomorrow. Mr. O'Malley has left some cash for you, to keep you going before the bank account is sorted out. I have my bridge club, if you don't mind my not coming."

"I'll be fine," said Flora. "I have to start sometime."

"Start what?"

"Start standing on my own two feet. You see, I can't remember when I last bought something. It must have been years ago."

The aunt smiled. "You'll find things are a bit more expensive, I'm afraid."

She wore the beige bombazine dress to go shopping. She took the train into Glasgow, relishing the novelty of travelling by herself and not in a group of nuns and schoolgirls, as she had done for the last ten years. It was a strange feeling—one of almost physical lightness. And in the shop she found herself overwhelmed by the choices available. In the convent one got by with very few things, and with virtually no choice. Now she was confronted with a bewildering range of outfits, the elegance of which only underlined the shabbiness of what she was wearing.

Mr. O'Malley had left what struck her as a grossly excessive amount of money, but by lunchtime she had spent most of what was in her purse. Many of the items would be delivered later, but the bombazine dress was now safely folded away in a cardboard box and she was wearing a new bright red dress, a patterned coat, a hat with a side peak, and a pair of high-heeled shoes, her first pair of high heels since university days. She felt slightly insecure in them, and almost lost her balance when crossing a road, but she would persist, and she was already feeling more confident about them.

Her aunt examined the new outfits and expressed pleasure.

"Very elegant," she said.

"Good," said Flora.

"And what plans have you for tomorrow?" asked the aunt.

"Edinburgh," said Flora. "I thought I might take a train to Edinburgh."

"And visit the museum?" asked the aunt.

"Possibly," said Flora. "But perhaps not this time." That was not what she would do; she had other plans altogether.

4

The convent had few mirrors and Flora was not accustomed to admiring herself. That morning, though, as she prepared to leave her aunt's house, she paused in front of the full-length dressing mirror on the front of her wardrobe. The person looking back at her was a stranger, or so it seemed to her, so accustomed had she become to the unchanging black and white garb of the last ten years. Now there was colour: the red of her new dress from Copeland's in Sauchiehall Street; the russet and purple of the coat she had agonised over for so long before buying; the violet of the close-fitting, rather jaunty hat. Was that really her—Flora Marshall, the same Flora Marshall who only a week ago had been standing in front of a class of Senior Four girls explaining calculus to them, hoping that they would grasp what she was trying to convey? Telling Jean Abercrombie not to fiddle with her ruler; looking askance at Jennifer Morris, who was clearly thinking about boys because that particular expression—the one she had on her face at the moment—was exactly what these Senior Four girls looked like when they thought about boys, which she believed was remarkably often; warning Natalie MacNeil that if she continued to talk to Margaret Cousins she would be sent to stand outside for ten minutes? That was not much of a sanction on the face of it, but what if Mother Superior walked past—and she was inclined to prowl—and saw them? That was the real threat.

She smiled at the thought. Sister Frances would have assumed responsibility for all that; Sister Frances, who had gasped with the shock of her announcement that she was leaving and had put her hand to her mouth as she had muttered, "May the Lord preserve us . . ." But then she had composed herself and said, as bravely as she could, "If the Lord wants me to take over Senior Four mathematics, then he must have his reasons." Poor Sister Frances—a good soul, she had always felt—would never have a red dress like this or a violet hat; or any hat, for that matter. Poor Sister Frances would never board a train to Edinburgh, by herself, in high heels, with the capital waiting for her with all its possibilities and delights; poor Sister Frances would never savour the wicked but delicious sensation of contemplating Protestantism. And Father Sullivan could look at her reproachfully for as long as he liked, she was beyond his reach now. She imagined for a moment what she might say to Father Sullivan were she to meet him in Sauchiehall Street; she in her new finery and he in his accustomed black. Their conversation, she imagined, would be superficial and restrained; Father Sullivan was unfailingly polite. But then she might steer it in a more engaging direction and say something like, "Tell me, Father, I've never really asked you this, but what's your view on the Reformation? Do you think it was timely, or even overdue?"

She turned away from the mirror, and blushed. These thoughts were unworthy of her. Father Sullivan had been kind to her; it was quite wrong to heap on his shoulders any abuses that the Church might have been guilty of in the past; it was quite wrong to imply that the need for the Reformation was in some way his responsibility, as if he had asked for a reformation because of the way he had tolerated sixteenth-century clerical wrongdoing. Nor should she dwell on the thought of Sister Frances doing what she herself had been doing for all those years. There was nothing dishonourable in being called to educate Senior Four: quite the contrary, in fact—it was an entirely worthy thing to devote one's life to the dispelling of ignorance. Girls were not born with a knowledge of trigonometry; they did not naturally understand what sines, cosines, and tangents were. It was a shameful thing, she decided, to revel in the distinction between her current position of freedom and the position she had been in only a few days ago.

She looked back into the mirror and thought: *A Protestant is looking back at me.* And as she boarded the train at Queen Street Station, carefully, as her new high-heeled shoes were taking a bit of getting used to, she thought: *Here's a Protestant boarding the train.*

She rolled the word around in her mouth, silently, without actually saying it out loud: *Protestant. Protestant.* It was one of those words that one uttered without thinking about what it really meant or where it came from. Protestants were the *other*; they were the people one did not marry; the people who supported Rangers rather than Celtic on the football field; they were the people who led godless, sometimes even sinful lives, doing what they wanted to do without any fear of the consequences for their immortal souls; Protestants were people who had fun . . . The last conclusion came unbidden. No, it could not be right—it had slipped out.

Protestants *protested*. They did not accept things as they were. They said no to corruption and vainglory; they said no to status and hierarchy; they stood up and made their protest. *Protestant*.

The train journey from Glasgow took not much more than an hour. They stopped at small stations on the way—Falkirk, Linlithgow—and various Protestants (they must be, she thought) got off the train, or boarded it. They sat down and read their papers or snatched a few minutes' sleep before arriving in Edinburgh. They are not thinking the sort of thoughts I'm thinking, she told herself. They don't know that I'm really Sister Flora underneath this red dress and violet hat—or have been Sister Flora for years—and that I'm heading to Edinburgh because I've decided that I want to start living, and it's easier to start living in another place, where people don't know you and have no preconceptions as to what you are like. In Glasgow she would always be Sister Flora, one of the nuns, one of the teachers at St. Catherine's; in Edinburgh she would be Flora Marshall, a woman in a violet hat, who had views and interests all of her own, a woman quite willing to enjoy the company of men, provided, of course, they were the right sort of men—men interested in conversation and the arts; and Edinburgh was full of such men, she believed.

At Waverley Station she made her way from the train towards the steps that led up to Princes Street. As she crossed the station concourse, under the sign that invoked the blessing of White Horse whisky, a shaft of light slanting down from the glass roof illuminated her progress, as a light falling from the sky might bathe a figure in a painting or stained-glass window, might fall on one who has been chosen for special attention, shown to us as a person who is about to do something significant, or be vouchsafed some special sign of favour. She was aware of the light about her; she felt its distant, attenuated warmth, and for a short while she hesitated, if only to savour the moment, conscious of the significance of what she was doing, feeling that she had somehow arrived at the point where an old life was consigned to the past and an entirely different life was being embarked upon. In this second life there would be new friends, and these would be people of her choosing, not just those with whom she happened to have grown up; there would be new people whose experience was quite different from her own, who had been to places she had never visited, who had insights into things she had never encountered, whose company would broaden her perspective beyond anything she had known before.

She imagined that there were people who, if they started a new life, would be keen to hide or ignore the life they had led before. Those with social ambitions might do that sort of thing, she thought; might conceal their origins, or embroider a modest past, could even deny their parents and family. She had heard people talk about instances of that and had shared their distaste for such behaviour. She would not seek to disguise the fact that she had been a nun; indeed, in the circles in which she was planning to move, such a past might even seem exotic, might be an advantage. *This is Flora—she was a nun, would you believe it? Yes, a nun!* It would be like having served in the Foreign Legion or having lived somewhere remote and romantic. Who was that man, the father of one of her past Senior Four girls, who had been pointed out to her by Sister Frances at some school function? Who was said by Sister Frances to have lived in Biarritz? Biarritz—people must live in Biarritz, but what an aura it gave them. They must live ordinary lives at one level; they must get colds and go to the shops and do the laundry and so on, but then all of this happened in *Biarritz,* and that somehow transformed it.

She reached the steps and started her climb up to Princes Street. A man brushed past her; he is in a hurry to get to the office, she thought, and he must be forgiven if he fails to apologise, as I am making my way up these steps far too slowly—in these heels—and he has somebody waiting for him at the other end, waiting and looking at his watch; but then the man stopped and raised his hat to her. He said, "I'm sorry—I wasn't looking where I was going." He spoke quietly, in what her mother would have described as an educated voice, and he smiled at her, revealing that one of his front teeth had been capped in gold—*educated teeth,* she thought, and returned his smile. But then he was gone, and she didn't have the opportunity to follow up their brief encounter with some further remark, such as: "Yes, of course, we are all in a hurry these days, aren't we?" *As if we had not been in such a hurry in 1959 or 1960 . . .* To say we were all in a hurry was a simple comment, but it conveyed so much, including regret at having spent ten years teaching Senior Four mathematics and trying to stop them thinking about boys all the time. Mind you, she thought, Senior Four could do to contemplate the folly of spending a whole year—admittedly not ten, but still a whole year—thinking about boys.

5

Opposite the monument to Sir Walter Scott stood Jenners, the finest department store that Edinburgh could muster, as confident in itself as any such store could be, as all-encompassing, as tempting. She took a deep breath as she entered its front door, reminding herself that she was as entitled as anybody to shop in this place—more so, perhaps, as she had in her purse slightly over two hundred pounds in crisp Bank of Scotland notes: the balance of the float that Mr. O'Malley had left with the aunt. It was a vast sum, she felt—thirty pounds would have more than done, but she had decided that after ten years of spending nothing she could perhaps indulge herself. It occurred to her now that nobody else in Jenners would have two hundred pounds in her purse, and that she could hold her head high amongst any grand Edinburgh ladies. She immediately thought: *Pride!* and made a conscious effort to exclude such thoughts. She would, as penance, send a cheque for twenty pounds to the St. Vincent de Paul Society once her cheque book arrived; that was the least she could do. *Penance*: Would that notion remain with her for life—even if she became a Protestant? The thought brought a moment of gloom: *You can take the girl out of the Church but you can't take the Church out of the girl.* They used to say that when they discussed girls who had strayed, and now she found herself applying the adage to herself. She swallowed hard. I am *not* Sister Flora, she muttered. I am no longer that person.

She stopped at the perfume counter, where a woman in a black wool dress with a white lace collar showed her the latest offering from Paris. She bought a small square bottle, trying, but failing, to conceal her surprise at the cost. The woman noticed, and smiled apologetically. "I know," she said. "But it's the ambergris, I believe."

She hesitated, feeling the heavy cut-glass bottle. Ambergris was something to do with whales, and she was not sure what bearing whales had on perfume. "I don't mind," she said. "If you like something enough, then the price is always worth it."

She thought: What grounds do I have for saying that—I, who have bought *nothing* for years, and *never* bought perfume?

There were other purchases, a pair of shoes, a blouse, a mohair cardigan, an Italian leather purse to replace the functional one lent her by her aunt. The Bank of Scotland notes, barely depleted, were tucked safely into this new purse and the battered older one tucked into the bag containing the shoes.

Now the tea room beckoned. She knew of Jenners tea room—it was legendary, even in Glasgow, and stood for everything that was refined and grand in Edinburgh. Tea at Jenners was not to be taken lightly, but seriously and with good intentions.

She was met by a young man in a morning suit, his hair smoothed down with pomade, the creases of his trousers knife-sharp. "I'm terribly sorry," he said, "but we don't have any tables free at the moment."

She surveyed the tea room and its sea of heads. She noticed the hats, and was relieved that she was wearing her own violet one.

"Oh dear."

The young man craned his neck to look for a table that he might have missed. "We're much busier than usual," he said, "except at the sales, of course; it's even busier then."

Two women nearby saw what was happening, and one of

them called the young man over. When he returned he was smiling. "Those two ladies wondered whether you would care to join them," he said. "They have a spare place."

She looked in their direction. Her eye was caught by one of the women, who smiled and pointed at the empty chair.

"Thank you," she said. "I shall be delighted."

She handed her parcels to the young man for safekeeping and made her way over to the table.

"You're very kind," she said. "I don't want to intrude."

"Not at all," said one of the women. "There's no point in having an empty chair, I always say."

"I've never seen it this crowded," said the other.

"Except at the sales," said Flora.

"Of course. Except at the sales."

They introduced one another. Her two new companions were called Helena and Marjorie. They were cousins, they explained. Helena lived in the country while Marjorie lived in the New Town. They met at the tea room every other Monday, they said.

They looked at her expectantly, waiting for her to tell them something about her. She noticed their surreptitious glance at her left hand, and guessed—correctly—the reason.

"I'm from Glasgow," she said.

"How nice," said Marjorie.

"Yes," said Helena. "How very nice."

This was followed by a silence.

"I was a teacher," Flora continued. "I only gave it up about ten days ago. I taught mathematics to girls." She did not say where.

"It's such an important subject," said Marjorie. "I was hopeless at it, although my husband is pretty good. He's an actuary. That's all mathematics, I think."

"And luck," said Helena.

The waiter came to take Flora's order.

"The sandwiches look particularly good today," said Helena. "But they always do."

Flora ordered a pot of tea and a plate of sandwiches.

"You've come to Edinburgh to do some shopping?" asked Helena.

Flora looked up at the ornate ceiling. She did not enjoy small talk; she never had. And now, quite suddenly, she felt the need to talk about something that mattered. She turned to Helena. "Actually," she said, "I've come over to Edinburgh in the hope that I might meet a man."

It was so easy to say, and yet so utterly shocking. She

felt as if she had impulsively stripped herself and was now naked. It was an extraordinary feeling—to say something so utterly shameless, in these surroundings, and in the company of two women whom she had only just met. That feeling of liberation that she had experienced on a number of occasions since leaving the convent, that light-headed sensation of release, now came back to her. It was an outrageous thing to say, but it was completely honest. That was what had been in the back of her mind all along. She might call it a shopping trip, but it was far more than that, and she might as well confess it.

For a moment neither of the other women said anything. Then Helena burst out laughing.

"Did I hear correctly?" she said. "Did you say you'd come to Edinburgh to find a man?"

Flora nodded. "That's exactly what I said."

Now Marjorie giggled. "Well, at least you're honest."

"Yes," said Helena. "Most of us are . . ."

". . . dishonest about that sort of thing," finished Marjorie.

"Exactly," said Helena.

Flora saw that there was real warmth in their smiles. "I know," she said. "You see, I was a nun for ten years."

Helena gasped. "An actual nun? The real thing?"

"Yes. It was a teaching order. I was Sister Flora. But I decided that I'd had enough."

They were staring at her open-mouthed. "Please forgive us," said Marjorie, "but it's not every day one goes to Jenners tea room and meets somebody who was a nun and who's now looking for a man."

"Exactly," said Helena.

Marjorie leaned forward. "I hope you don't mind my asking," she said, "but how are you planning to meet this man?"

Flora thought for a moment. It was a morning for honesty, and she would not pretend to have a plan when she had none. "I have no idea," she said. "I've never really thought about it."

Helena and Marjorie exchanged glances.

"You see," said Marjorie, "it's not all that easy . . . We know a lot about it, you see." She glanced again at Helena, who nodded encouragement. "Helena and I are both currently without husbands."

"Mine died," said Helena, "and Marjorie's just, well . . ."

"Went off with another woman," said Marjorie. "They do that, you see—they go off if you're unlucky."

"Water under the bridge," said Helena.

"Yes," agreed Marjorie. "No sense in dwelling on the past." Then she added, "She was a little strumpet, you know. And interested in one thing, and one thing alone."

"Two things, if you count money," added Helena.

They were silent as the waitress brought Flora's tea and a large plate of sandwiches.

"I can't eat all of those myself," said Flora. "I hope that you'll help me."

Both Helena and Marjorie took a sandwich before Flora had a chance to help herself.

"So kind of you," said Helena.

"Yes," said Marjorie. "So kind."

"Marjorie may have some ideas," said Helena, through a mouthful of egg sandwich. "She's very good at doing these things."

"What things?" asked Flora.

"Finding suitable men," answered Helena. "Arranging little lunch parties."

"I enjoy it," said Marjorie. "I've successfully brought together three couples over the last eighteen months. That's a better record than some professionals have."

"Professionals who run marriage bureaux," explained Helena. "Sometimes those places make grossly exaggerated claims. They charge ridiculous fees and then they come up with some very unpromising material."

Flora wondered why Marjorie had not yet found a man for herself if she was so good at it. "But in your case?" she said, looking at Marjorie.

"Oh, I'm extremely fussy," said Marjorie, quite cheerfully. "I'm looking for a particular sort of man—and I'm in no hurry."

"Whereas I am," said Flora, half-seriously.

Marjorie wiped a crumb off her lips. "It so happens that I'm having a little lunch party today."

Helena looked at her watch. "Oh, come on, darling: it's half past ten already."

"It would be no trouble to lay an extra place," said Marjorie. She looked at Flora. "Would you like that, Miss Marshall?"

"Flora, please," said Flora, remembering just in time not to say Sister Flora.

"Would you like that, Flora?"

Flora hesitated. She was not sure that she was ready. It was easy enough to talk about meeting men, but the actual business of speaking to them was quite another matter. She was not even sure what one talked to men about. She could say a lot about Senior Four and their problems, but would men be interested in hearing about the little ways of schoolgirls? Even some of the racier bits?

She made up her mind. "Yes, please—if it's no trouble. I should hate to be any trouble."

"None at all," said Marjorie. "But we'd better get along, I think. I have a maid, but she needs to be supervised—you know how these women are."

Flora nodded. "Oh yes," she said. *You don't,* she said to herself. *You have been a servant yourself. Remember that.*

She paid the bill for all three of them, and left a handsome tip.

"Very generous," said Helena, eyeing the tip. "But one should be careful not to encourage excessive expectations."

Flora noticed that Marjorie's eyes had been fixed on the new wallet, the bulging wad of Bank of Scotland notes having caught her attention. She thought for a moment, and then said, "My ship has come in. I had an uncle over near Greenock. He left me everything, you see."

"Ah," said Helena.

"You're very lucky," said Marjorie. "That should make it much easier to find a man—much, much easier."

"Marjorie, darling!" scolded Helena.

"But it's a truth universally acknowledged," said Marjorie lightly. "Jane Austen would have understood perfectly."

"Perhaps," said Helena. "But I'm not altogether convinced that we should always reveal everything we have in mind."

"Oh, nonsense!" said Marjorie, and smiled mischievously at Flora.

I'm so glad I've found you, thought Flora.

As they left the tea room, Marjorie whispered to her, "You know, Flora, men must like you—with your looks."

This came as a surprise. "I'm not sure . . ."

"No need for false modesty," said Marjorie. "You're a very beautiful woman, you know. Men will not be indifferent to that."

She floundered. She had never thought about her looks—or, at least, not for a long time. "I don't know about that," she said at last.

"Well, I do," said Marjorie. "And I'm telling you. You are not going to find this difficult. Quite the opposite, in fact. You'll be fighting them off, my dear."

Helena had overheard this. "Marjorie is rarely wrong," she said.

6

The lunch party was held in Marjorie's house in Great King Street. This was a Georgian town house, one room wide but with four floors and a basement. The dining room gave off a large drawing room, both with floor-to-ceiling windows into which light flooded from both north and south. On the walls of the drawing room were several Scots colourist paintings, lively to the point of exuberance, adding splashes of red and yellow.

The maid had wasted time polishing silver, with the result that the cooking was behind schedule.

"Look at us," said Marjorie, glaring at the maid. "Completely unprepared."

Helena and Flora both helped—Flora peeling potatoes for the salad while Helena arranged plates of cold meat and cheese.

"Five guests," said Marjorie, reeling off a list of names to which Helena responded with a nod or a shake of the head. There were four men and one woman. "I like to keep the odds in our favour," she continued. "I can't be doing with those occasions in which there are equal numbers of men and women. Why on earth do people do it? Can't they *count?*"

"To give everybody a chance," said Helena.

"Oh, nonsense," said Marjorie.

Flora wondered whether her new friend said *Oh, nonsense* to everything with which she disagreed. How she would have loved to say that to Mother Superior or Father Sullivan. The occasional *Oh, nonsense* would have stopped them in their tracks, but nobody dared, of course. It was Protestants who said *Oh, nonsense;* they had been saying that since the sixteenth century.

They were ready just in time.

"You see what I mean about her," whispered Marjorie, nodding in the direction of the kitchen stairs. "She had done nothing but polish the silver—of all things!"

"You'll have to get rid of her," said Helena. "You can't be held hostage to that sort of thing."

Marjorie looked at her watch. "Well, I'll think about it. The problem is: these people won't work."

Flora turned away. There was something about this whispered conversation that she did not like. She had exchanged no more than a few words with the maid, but they had smiled at one another and there had been a current of unspoken fellow-feeling. She had noticed that the maid had a rash on her wrist—some sort of skin complaint, she thought. Doing the washing up would not help that, she decided. There was a saint for skin disorders—Saint Lazarus, was it not? She could light a candle to Saint Lazarus . . . but then she remembered that candles were a thing of the past, and that if they were to be lit it would be by others; she would miss them, of course, as she always loved the smell they made when extinguished—a smell that was redolent of childhood and mystery and the love of her late parents whom she missed so sorely, even now.

One floor below, a doorbell rang. Marjorie brightened. "Alan Miller," she said. "I bet you ten shillings it's him. On the dot of one. He's like that German painter they used to set their watches by in Berlin. He always went for his walk at exactly the same time."

"Actually, darling," said Helena, "it was a philosopher. Immanuel Kant. And it was Königsberg, not Berlin."

Marjorie brushed aside the correction. "Be that as it may, the point remains—it'll be Alan, and Geoffrey Inver with him." She turned to Flora. "Alan is mid-forties, and so,

I believe, is Geoffrey. They've been sharing a flat for a long time—much cheaper that way. Gloucester Place. They're both lawyers, but different sorts of lawyers, I think. Very charming."

"They'd both make very good husbands," said Helena. "It's a pity one could only marry one of them—otherwise you'd be able to get two for the price of one."

Marjorie seemed shocked by this. "Helena, darling!"

"Just a joke," said Helena.

"Isn't it strange," said Marjorie, "how polygamy—where it's permitted—allows men to have multiple wives but does not allow women to have multiple husbands?"

"Would any woman want more than one husband?" asked Flora.

Helena laughed. "Good point," she said.

They heard voices on the stair. A few minutes later, ushered in by the maid, two men appeared.

"Darling!" said the taller of the men, stepping forward to embrace Marjorie. He kissed her on both cheeks. "And other darling," he said to Helena. "Every bit as lovely, of course."

He stopped at Flora. "And *who* have we here?"

Marjorie made the introductions. "Flora, this is Alan Miller. And this is Geoffrey Inver." The other man stepped forward and took Flora's hand. He inclined his head rather than trying to kiss her.

Marjorie continued. "Flora is from Glasgow."

"Glasgow!" exclaimed Alan. "How brave!"

"So near and yet so far," said Geoffrey, making a vague gesture with his right hand.

A further male guest arrived and then, shortly afterwards, another—accompanied by a woman. The man who came by himself was called Richard Snow. The other man was Thomas McGibbon, who arrived with a thin, rather nervous-looking woman in her forties who simply gave her name as Lizzie. "Lizzie is a sculptress," explained Marjorie in an aside to Flora. "Hence the intensity."

"Are they?" asked Flora, looking across the room at Lizzie.

"Are who what?"

"Sculptresses . . . are they intense?"

Marjorie looked at her as if she had asked the most obvious of questions. "But of course they are, dear. *Very* intense people, I've found."

Flora thought: *I've never met a sculptress. Here I am, thirty-two, and I've never met a sculptress.* She wondered what Sister Frances would make of a sculptress: they would be chalk and cheese, she thought, with poor Sister Frances's complete lack of intensity.

Marjorie gave everybody a glass of sherry and then, fifteen minutes later, announced, *"Alla tavola!"* Flora smiled: she could work out what that meant, although she had never heard it before. So that was what people said in sophisticated circles: *alla tavola*.

They sat down. She found herself with Richard Snow on her right and Geoffrey Inver on her left. Geoffrey spoke to her first, as they started the soup.

"So," he said. "Glasgow."

As he spoke, she noticed that a small rivulet of courgette soup dribbled down his chin; soup was a challenge to some people, she thought: *sent by the Lord to try us*, as Sister Beatrice was fond of saying of any irritation, from traffic lights to the more recalcitrant members of Senior Four.

She was not sure how to respond to Geoffrey Inver, but decided to say, "Yes." It was not enough, she felt, for somebody simply to say "Glasgow" and leave it at that.

It was as if he realised that himself. "I must spend more time in Glasgow," he said. "There it is, only forty miles away, and one spends so little time there. Perhaps next year. Who knows?"

"There's a lot going on in Glasgow," said Flora.

Geoffrey nodded. "So they say."

"There's the Citizens' Theatre," she ventured. She had never been there. Nuns did not go to the Citizens' Theatre, but for a few moments she imagined Mother Superior sitting in the front row with Father Sullivan on one side of her and Sister Frances on the other. Poor Sister Frances would have difficulty understanding the play and would have to have it explained to her by Father Sullivan, who had a reputation for being able to make things understandable.

She continued a desultory conversation with Geoffrey, but realised that he was bored. At first she was discouraged, but then she thought: *What does it matter if he finds me boring? What does his own life amount to? Being a lawyer in Edinburgh, going to lunch parties like this? What's so special about that?*

She was able to turn to Richard Snow once the soup plates had been taken away. He seemed keen to engage in conversation, beginning by asking her how she knew Marjorie. "Jenners," she replied, without thinking much about it. She had not intended it to be taken as a witty answer, but it was.

He smiled. "That's the place to meet," he said. "I can imagine people saying to themselves: 'Oh, I need to go and buy a pair of socks and make a few new friends—I must go to Jenners.'"

She laughed. "It wasn't quite like that."

"Of course not."

She looked sideways at him; a quick look of appraisal. He was forty-something, she thought, and he had weathered well. His complexion was tanned and healthy—as if he enjoyed hill-walking or sailing, or something else that took him out into the open air. Her gaze slipped to his left hand: there was no ring.

He asked her what she did.

"I used to teach," she said.

"What a wonderful job."

She was surprised, but pleased at his response. "Sometimes," she said.

"I wouldn't have the patience," he said.

"They can try such patience as one has," she said, thinking of Senior Four, and of Natalie MacNeil in particular. She hesitated, and then continued, "There's a girl called Natalie MacNeil. She tried my patience more than any of the others. Dreadful girl." It was strangely liberating to describe Natalie MacNeil in this way, even if it was distinctly uncharitable.

He laughed. "I think I can picture her rather well. But what was the problem?"

"Boys," said Flora, feeling slightly daring. She had never before had a conversation like this with a man—Father Sullivan, of course, did not count. "Her mind was full of boys."

"Ah," said Richard Snow, smiling.

They continued their conversation through the main course and into the dessert. Then, when they left the table for coffee, Richard Snow said, "Let's go and sit by the window."

He told her what he did. "I have a small shipping firm," he said. "It's very small beer as these things go. We have five vessels—that's all."

She asked him where they went.

"They're very unadventurous," he said. "Glasgow to Hamburg. Leith to Stavanger. That sort of thing. We don't go far."

"Do you suffer from sea-sickness?" she asked.

He laughed. "I don't actually go on the ships themselves," he said. "I arrange the cargoes—that sort of thing."

She noticed the colour of his eyes, which was an attenuated hazel. She liked them. For his part, he was taken with her nose. It was perfectly proportioned, he thought. Some noses were just right—they were the right size and in the right place. Flora's was such a nose.

He said to her, "It's Sunday tomorrow."

"Yes."

"Have you ever been to the Botanical Gardens here in Edinburgh?"

She shook her head. She had visited so few places.

"I wondered whether you might care to come with me there tomorrow? There's going to be one of their lectures. One of the keepers is going to be talking about cactuses."

"Cactuses!"

He smiled encouragingly. "I know not everyone's interested in cactuses."

"But I am," she assured him. "They're fascinating plants." Poor Sister Frances had kept a cactus in a pot near her window. It had never flowered, although Sister Bernadette had said it would. "Sometimes they flower only every ten years," she had explained.

"Well, then, you might find it interesting."

"Yes, I'd very much like to come with you. Thank you."

"Not at all." He looked up at the ceiling. "Half past eleven? Where are you staying?"

She thought quickly. "The North British Hotel." It was

directly above the station; she had seen it when she went up the steps. She would go back to Jenners, buy what she needed for an overnight stay, and then telephone her aunt to say that she was going to spend the night in Edinburgh. She had never stayed in a hotel before—not once—and the idea was strongly appealing. Why should she not? She had more than enough money to stay in any hotel she chose. She was free and she could do exactly as she wished. She liked Richard Snow and, she had decided, he showed every sign of enjoying her company. So it was not all that hard to find a man. On the contrary: she had come to Edinburgh and had found one within hours—a good-looking man with hazel eyes and an interest in cactuses. What more could anybody want?

"I could come and pick you up at the hotel," he said. "We'll drive down there."

"Thank you. You said eleven thirty?"

"Yes . . ." He hesitated. "I might be a little bit late—no more than five or ten minutes. I shall be at Mass, you see."

She caught her breath, but only for the shortest moment. It was a sign, or perhaps an enquiry. Was he testing her for prejudice—or for suitability? *I'm not a Protestant,* she thought. *I never even reached the start line.* It was destiny, she thought, and one should never fight destiny. Go along with it, and with the tides that carry you through life. They know where you're going, and you do not. And then she thought: Some embraces last for life. Curiously enough, this realisation did not depress her; it was what she had rather expected.

"I could meet you there. What are the times?"

She saw the relief in his reaction. *Destiny,* she said to herself.

She went back to Jenners, bought what she needed, and then walked the short distance to the North British Hotel. They had plenty of rooms, and they gave her a suite overlooking Princes Street. She sat there, her feet propped up on a stool. She ordered a half-bottle of champagne, which was brought up to her room by a smartly attired young man. The young man opened the champagne bottle for her and gave her a look. It was not a look that she understood, but it had a flirtatious feel to it. Men, it seemed, were plentiful, once one started to search for them. Indeed, she thought, Marjorie was right: one had to fight them off—or at least some of them.

She sent him away. She closed her eyes. Such happiness, she thought; such happiness came from knowing who you were and where you came from. And from knowing, too, that you did not have to go back unless you really wanted to, and sometimes you did.

I

"He was very proud of being Scottish, you know."

She touched the photograph gently, as one might touch something precious. The young man sitting opposite her, on the other side of the card table on which the photographs had been spread out, noticed that there was sun damage to her hands. Or was it those discolourations that people called *liver spots*? No, it was most likely the sun, because it was fierce here in southern Tuscany, and the summer months—of which this was one—could be oven-like, even here in the hills, where it was meant to be cooler because of the Apennine wind. On the way up the winding road from San Casciano dei Bagni he had passed a sign that warned of snow—inconceivable now, in this heat, but presumably a real enough issue in winter.

"Yes, very proud," she continued. "Not in an embarrassing way, of course. He often wore a kilt—just as he's doing in this photograph. But he didn't go on about Scotland as some people do. I think that's boastful, don't you? To go on at length about your country and its merits. Boastful and distasteful, too, because going on about one's country often involves adverse comparisons with other countries, don't you think?"

The young man nodded. "Countries and football teams . . ."

She laughed. "I suspect you don't take much interest in football, do you? No, I thought not." She paused. "But being proud of *being* something is rather odd, I've always thought. It's rather like being proud of being tall. How can you be proud of something that had absolutely nothing to do with any effort or talent on your part? Frankly, I don't see it."

"No, probably not."

"You can be relieved, I suppose, that you were born something or other—American, say—but that's not the same thing as being proud. You can be thankful that your parents reached America in time for you to be born there—and I suppose a lot of people were grateful for that—but you can't claim any credit for it."

"They could, though."

She frowned. "Who could?"

"The people who reached America. They could be proud of being American."

"Yes, of course. But that pride would be about what they had achieved. They got there, and they could feel proud of that. That's legitimate enough, but it only works for the first generation."

"I see what you mean." He touched his forehead. It was hot and he felt damp. "You're Scottish too," he said.

She smiled, and sat back in her chair. He noticed that the hem of the skirt she was wearing had become unstitched. Age could bring neglect of one's clothes—a giving up, really—but then he reminded himself she was only sixty-three and that was hardly all that old. He himself would be sixty-three in exactly thirty years' time. And that would be in—he did the mental arithmetic quickly—two thousand and three. He thought: Would they say *twenty three* in the way in which we said nineteen seventy-three? He thought it unlikely. It would have to be something like *twenty oh-three*. Stands the calendar at twenty oh-three and is there honey still for tea? Nobody would remember Rupert Brooke by then. Nor have tea, with bread and honey. There used to be a country called England . . .

He was aware she was talking. He had been momentarily back in Cambridge, sitting in his room, waiting for his friends to come back from the river.

"I am," she said, "although people often didn't realise it. Harry and I, you see, were both taken to be English because of the way we spoke. We didn't have a Scottish accent because our class—and I'm sorry to have to use such an objectionable term, but there is no other way of saying it—because our class was brought up to speak in the same way as a certain sort of English person. That's an old story in Scotland, the rejection of the Scots tongue, but it did happen. We started to spurn our own language, even if we kept a few words as mementos, so to speak. Words like *dreich* that we use as occasional shibboleths. That's another interesting word, isn't it? The shibboleth was your password to whatever you wanted to get into—or out of. I suppose you had to use the shibboleth to avoid being stoned or put to the sword, or something of that nature.

"Maybe it was because of that problem of misidentification that he made much of being Scottish. And it can't have helped to be sent off to that school in Perthshire that pretended to be English."

She had been looking out of the window as she spoke; now she looked at him.

"I'm so sorry," she said. "How tactless of me. You probably went to one of those places yourself."

He reassured her that he had not taken offence. "I went to school in England. A place called Marlborough," he said.

She nodded. "You were at the Courtauld Institute, weren't you?"

"Yes."

"You studied under the Poussin man . . . what was he called?"

"Blunt. Anthony Blunt. I didn't know him all that well. I found him rather formal in his manner."

She smiled. "Like a painting by Poussin?"

"Yes, you could say that. There's a reason why we like this artist rather than that one."

He picked up the photograph again. "May I?"

"Of course. I should put them in a proper album, but there's something depressing about putting photographs away. It's rather like filing something that shouldn't be filed—like reducing something full of meaning and association to a . . . to a specimen. As lepidopterists do."

He laughed. "We all have a slight tendency to lepidoptery."

He examined the photograph more closely.

"That's you holding the pony, I take it? And that's him in his kilt." He paused. "What on earth is he riding?"

"It was a sort of tricycle," she explained. "It was a museum piece even then—it had belonged to his father as a boy. I remember it squeaking terribly."

"And the other little girl?"

"She was their farm manager's daughter. She was always hanging about, hoping we'd play with her."

"He looks very unhappy about something."

She smiled. "He probably thought I was trying to push him around. I thought he was stubborn—I couldn't understand why boys seemed so unwilling to do as they were told." She glanced at her visitor. "On the subject of happiness, how ubiquitous do you think unhappiness is today?"

He was unprepared for the question. "I'm not sure if I know how to answer that."

"What I mean is this: Are we happier today because we know a lot more than we knew then? Are we happier because Freud came along and showed us why we were making ourselves unhappy? Are we happier because of the sexual revolution?" She paused, and looked out of the window again. "Out there—in Italy—are people happier because they can say boo to the local priest? I think they are."

He ventured an opinion. "The Italians seem to have been happy in spite of religion."

"Or because of it? Remember that Catholicism is only marginally about guilt. For the rest it's cheerfully pagan—plaster saints, miracles, superstition, feast days. People love ceremony, and there's bags of ceremony and dressing up in Catholicism."

She picked up the photograph again. "Look at him," she said fondly. "Look at me. Fifty-whatever years ago, when it was all about to begin.

"And that hat I'm wearing," she mused. "I was so proud of it. It was a great, floppy thing. I've been carrying that hat with me—metaphorically, of course—for decades, for all my adult life." She pointed to it. Her expression was one that he found hard to interpret. Resentment? Regret? "We carry with us the clothes of childhood, don't we? We keep them on long after they have ceased to fit."

He looked at her with sympathy. "Yes," he said. "I haven't heard it put that way before, but yes."

She became brisk. "May I ask you something, Mr. Summers? This article you're writing for *The Burlington Magazine?*"

"Yes?"

"What exactly is it?"

"It's a profile. As you probably know, *The Burlington*'s period is usually somewhat earlier. We do very little on twentieth-century artists. But in his case, the editor thought it appropriate, because of the neo-classical nature of the later work."

She sounded slightly impatient. "Yes, I understand all that. What I want to know is this: Are you going to be kind to Harry?"

The question seemed to surprise him. "But of course we are. It's a tribute, really."

"Because so many things you read now are infected with a spirit of unkindness. People feel they have to show how clever they are by debunking others—by belittling them."

"I would never do that. I give you my word."

She smiled. "The fact that nobody says *I give you my word* any more tells me all I need to know about you. And I trust you."

"I have nothing but admiration for his work. I have no other motive."

"In that case, I can tell you the story that nobody else knows. You may or may not wish to mention it in your . . . your profile. But it's the key to everything."

"Then I'm very grateful to you. I'd like you to know that."

She barely acknowledged his thanks. "Look at the photograph," she said. "I'll start from there."

"Do you mind if I make notes?"

"No, that's what you people do. You have to take notes."

He began to write as she talked. Later he wrote it out,

at far greater length than was required for his article, filling in the details of how he imagined the protagonists thought, of how they felt. It became a story in its own right; his version of what must have transpired. An omniscient narrator, were he or she to read what he wrote, would say, "Yes, that is exactly right. That is exactly how it happened." For it was.

2

The photograph was taken in Argyll, he wrote, on one of those mountainous peninsulas on the western edge of Scotland. In the nineteenth century it was fashionable to put the proceeds of money made elsewhere—from all the pain and exploitation that lay behind Victorian fortunes—into the construction of large houses, inserted into the wildly romantic Scottish landscape. Remote glens, stripped of their human population during the Highland Clearances of the previous century, now became the backdrop to stone-built fantasies, complete with turrets and towers. Scots baronial, a whole new architectural style, evolved to cater for this enthusiasm—and its accompanying pretensions. On that particular peninsula, an adventurer who had made his fortune in the goldfields of southern Africa built a rambling and unlikely castle solely for the use of his guests, an affirmation in stone of the sheer power of money.

More modest houses—still large, though—met the needs of smaller landed proprietors. These people did not aspire to vast estates; they were drawn from professional and business circles in Edinburgh or Glasgow, or farther afield, that fancied a toehold in the Highlands. They spent the summer months there engaged in country pursuits, before leaving in the autumn when the gales swept in from the Atlantic. They regarded themselves as a race apart from the locals, to whom they condescended as parvenus have always condescended to the people of the places they choose to colonise.

Their families were neighbours, even if they lived three miles apart: houses, particularly large ones, were few and far between in the Highlands. His father, an Edinburgh banker, was called Struan; his mother, the daughter of an English general who served most of his career in India, was called Phyllis. They never saw the general, who preferred to spend his leave in Simla. It was widely understood that he drank, but then that was not unusual. Phyllis had not seen her father since the age of sixteen, when she had made the long journey to India, became sick shortly after arrival, and had then been sent home virtually by return. She stayed with an aunt in Bristol until, at the age of twenty-one, she married Struan, whom she had met at the Caledonian Ball in London.

In 1920 she gave birth to Harry. He was her only child and she lavished affection upon him. "I want so much for him," she said to one of her Edinburgh friends, but when asked what it was that she wanted, she could think of no answer. It would seem too vague to say that she hoped he would be happy; she wanted that, of course, but there was far more to her feelings than that. She wanted greatness.

"Perhaps you want to protect him from the world," said the friend. "You want him to be safe."

"Let him be what he chooses to be," said Struan. "Boys . . . men . . . just like to be left alone."

This had led to the exchange of knowing glances between the women. "Do they now?" said Phyllis.

"Yes," said Struan. "That's what they like. They don't need to be watched over by women all the time."

She did not argue the point, but she knew she was right, and he was wrong. Boys—and men—needed women; they were lost without them. It was masked at times, of course, but the need was always there. Underneath all the bravado, men were little boys, whistling in the dark.

They sent him to school in Edinburgh, ignoring the general's suggestion that he be sent—at his expense—to a militaristic boarding school in Hampshire. "I don't want him to have an English education," said Struan. "He's my son. He's Scottish."

Phyllis was happy to side with her husband. She could not understand how people could send small children—seven- and eight-year-olds—to boarding school. "They're far too young to leave their mothers," she said. "It's a form of cruelty."

"Yes," said Struan. "But don't mollycoddle him."

She looked at him reproachfully. "I have no intention of doing that," she said. "None at all."

Towards the end of June each year they left their house in Edinburgh to make the journey to the house in Argyll, where they would spend two months. They travelled by train to Fort William, to be collected by their farm manager. He drove them back to the house along the tortuous road that wound along the edge of the peninsula, barely more than a track, and unused, even now, to vehicles. Harry pressed his face to the car window, drinking in the landscape of sweeping mountainsides and tumbling waterfalls. The farm manager talked on the journey about sheep and salmon fishing and the movement of the deer. There was discussion, in muted tones, of the loss of a local fishing boat. "Five bairns now without a father," said the manager. "Just like that."

"You'll be looking forward to seeing Jenny," said his mother, as the car made its way up the drive, through the profusion of rhododendrons.

"Nasty things," said his father—of the shrubs, still in riotous blossom. "A haven for midges. They should have left them where they found them—in the Himalayas."

"Beautiful," said his mother.

"You can't stop them," said the farm manager. "Once they take root, it's the devil's own job getting rid of them."

"Still beautiful," she said, and turning to Harry, "Jenny? Has she written to you? Are they up yet, do you know?"

The farm manager answered. "Arrived last week. He's laid up with his leg, I believe."

Harry tried to see through the rhododendrons, to the outcrop of rock that he knew they concealed, but there was only darkness. Jenny's father had been shot by a German—he knew that because he had heard the adults talking about it. *Did he shoot him back?* We don't think of it like that. *But why not?* Because we just don't. Because when there's a war, people are told to shoot the other side. It doesn't mean that they hate them as people. They're just doing their job as soldiers. *If anybody shot me, I'd shoot him back. As long as I wasn't dead, of course.*

"Your father," he had once said to Jenny, "has got a bullet in his leg, hasn't he?"

She had looked at him with tolerance. He was not to know. His own father had stayed in the bank. He knew nothing about the trenches. *The trenches* . . . The word, it seemed, had vast power in the adult world. Her father had been in the trenches when the German shot him.

"Of course he hasn't got a bullet in his leg, stupid! You can't walk if you have a bullet in your leg. In fact, you die because the bullet goes up your leg and into your heart. It goes through your veins. That happened to lots of people."

"Even if you got shot in the toe? Even then?"

This required thought. "Sometimes. Sometimes people died if they got shot in the toe. It depends on which toe. If it's just the little toe, then you may be all right. If it's your big toe, then you may not be so lucky."

"Then why didn't your father die?"

She sighed; he knew so little of what the world was really like. "He had an operation. In something called a field hospital. They took the bullet out and put it in a jar. I've seen it."

He was impressed. To have a father who had been shot by a German was distinction enough, but to have the very bullet in a jar put one in a very special position.

She looked at him. "My father won," she said.

"Won what?"

"The War. My father won the War."

He looked down at the ground. His father could have won it too, had he gone to the trenches. But somebody had to stay, his mother explained, because if they didn't stay to run the banks then there would be no money, and if there was no money then the Germans would have romped home to victory and that would have been the end of the British Empire. Which would have been like turning out the sun, she said. Just that: turning out the sun.

And now here was Mr. Currie having trouble with his leg, reminding everybody that you may win the War but you paid a price for it.

"All those names," his mother said, shaking her head as she showed him the simple war memorial that had been erected beside the kirk. "Every one of them. Every single one of them a hero. All ordinary boys from right here. Local families. Every one of them."

But now she said, as they approached the house, "Jenny

will come over, no doubt. They'll have seen the car. People know when you arrive. They don't in Edinburgh, do they? You could disappear into thin air and nobody would be any the wiser. But they know here."

3

She came to the house virtually every day. Sometimes he imagined he was by himself, engaged in some activity of his own devising, and then he would realise that she was there, almost as if she had been there all along, watching him, waiting for an opportunity to tell him that he was doing things the wrong way, or should be doing something else altogether.

For the most part, he was happy to follow her suggestions. "We could pretend we were Vikings," she said. "There were lots of them settled near here, you know. I could be a Viking lady and you could be a Viking warrior."

He liked the idea, but was uncertain what Vikings did.

"They mostly burn things," she said. "They travel in long boats—really long—and then they come ashore and burn everything. They carry everybody off."

"Where to?"

Her answer was vague. She pointed out towards the islands. "Over there. Maybe Skye. They liked Skye."

"And what did they do to them? Did they kill them?"

She shook her head. "Not always. The Vikings sometimes killed people—if they felt in the mood—but most of the time they just carried them off and overcame them. That was enough."

He was not sure how people were overcome, and asked for clarification, but she simply shook her head. "I'll tell you later," she said. "Not now."

He gathered an armful of brushwood from the woods above the house. They set fire to this down by the shore, the smoke billowing up voluminously. It was a convincing Viking display and he was momentarily awed by what they had done.

"That'll show all the Scottish people," she said. "They'll know that we're here. They'll run off from the Vikings, but we'll get them sooner or later."

"And overcome them?"

"Maybe." She thought for a moment, moving away from the smoke. He followed her; the smoke was making his eyes smart. "Have you heard of Somerled?"

He shook his head. She knew so much more than he did.

"He lived here a long time ago. He was Scottish, although his mother was a Viking. He rose up against the Vikings."

"Did they kill him?"

"No, he beat them. He showed the Scots how to overcome the Vikings." She paused. "I learned all that in history. You've got a lot to learn, Harry."

"I know."

"Still, you can pick up quite a lot from me. I can tell you quite a lot of what you have to know—just so that you won't seem so ignorant when you go to a bigger school. You don't want them to laugh at you."

"No, I don't."

"So you should just listen to me."

He said nothing. He had always listened to her, it seemed to him, and he would have to continue to do so.

"Let's go and catch some sheep," she said. "And eat them."

He stared at her open-eyed.

"We're Vikings," she reminded him. "Remember."

They ran towards a bedraggled ewe that had made its way down to the line of seaweed on the shore. The ewe had her lamb at her side—a cold year had made for spindly lambs—and she backed away in panic, the lamb bleating in confusion. For a moment he thought that Jenny had been serious, and that she would fall upon the ewe—would overcome it—but she stopped short of the frightened creature, waved her arms a final time, and watched as it scampered off to a safe distance.

"You see," she said. "Now we can go back to our Viking house."

This was a clearing they had made under a particularly thick rhododendron bush. They had brought in two hessian sacks, using one for a floor and one as a curtain. There was just enough room for them both to sit down.

She had brought sandwiches.

"Did Vikings eat sandwiches?" he asked.

"Yes, of course they did. They made sandwiches from the things they stole from the Scots. Then they ate them before the Scots could steal them back."

He bit into the sandwich. It was thick with the smoked salmon that Jenny's parents' housekeeper, Mrs. Macneill, made in the smoker at the back of her house. She soaked the salmon in rum and honey before lighting the fire, and this gave it a rich, rather sweet taste.

She looked at him. "When are you going away to school?" she asked. "Not in Edinburgh, but that other one—the one in Perthshire."

"Next year," he said. "Just before my twelfth birthday."

She considered this. "You could run away," she said. "If you don't like it, you could run away."

"Where?"

"Here. Or you could go to Glasgow, if you like. I know somewhere you could hide in Glasgow. I could bring you food, if you liked. Nobody would know."

He thought for a moment. "I might like that school."

She shook her head. "No, you won't. They beat you at boys' schools, you know. On your bottom. They have canes and things."

"That's only if you do something bad."

She denied this. "They beat you if they don't like your face," she said. "My cousin went to a school like that. They beat him because his face was too round."

"But he couldn't help that . . ."

"Of course he couldn't. But that didn't stop them from beating him. He hated it and he would have run away, only he was worried that if he ran away they would just beat him even more."

He was silent. The world, it seemed to him, was a place of dire and constant threat. There were Germans who would shoot you and there were others who would beat you. This made life an anxious, restless business. He wished that somehow it were different; that the world was a kinder, less threatening place. The problem, it seemed to him, was with boys and men. They were the ones who were cruel; they were the ones who made it hard to be a boy. Girls and women were different, and kinder. But there was not much you could do if nature decided that you were going to be a boy. You had to accept it. You had to work out how to survive, so that your chances of being beaten or shot were diminished. He was not sure how to do that yet, but he thought that he might learn.

It was Jenny's mother who realised that he could draw. She was an amateur watercolourist who painted the things that amateur watercolourists like to paint: hazy seascapes, hills covered in purple heather, the moods of the sky. She had a box of oil pastels that she allowed him to use, and the results intrigued her. He had sketched a domestic scene—a table covered with a gingham tablecloth, a teapot and cups, a chair with an intensely red cushion. She could see that he had an eye for colour, but there was more that that: he had composed his picture well.

"But that's remarkable, Harry," she said. "Who's taught you to draw so well?"

"Nobody," he said. "Nobody's taught me."

"I find that hard to believe. Are you sure?"

He nodded. "I like drawing."

Jenny joined in. "He's going to be a famous artist one day. I can tell that. I've known for ages."

He was embarrassed. "I'm not. I'm not all that good."

Jenny's mother brought out a book to show him. "I'm going to lend you this. There are lots of lovely pictures in it. They're all Dutch."

He opened the book, and ran his hand across one of the pages. There was a picture of peasants at a village feast.

"That's Breughel, I think," she said. "There were several Breughels—I get them a bit mixed up. Let me look. Yes, that's Peter Breughel, who started them off. What do you think of it?"

He studied the figures. "They're cooking a pig."

"Yes, they are. It must have been a very important celebration for them to cook a pig. I think they're looking forward to it."

He turned the page.

"That's what they call an interior," she said. "The Dutch loved painting scenes like that. And do you see something? You see that open doorway? The Dutch artists loved open doorways—it meant that you could look out of the painting *into* something. Here we're looking into a courtyard. And you see the sunlight. You see how clear it is outside? They liked that."

He touched the picture, which was reproduced in black and white. "I wish I could see the colours."

"When you get back to Edinburgh, you can go to the National Gallery. They have paintings like that. You can see the colours then."

He took the book away. He spent hours studying the pictures and trying to pronounce the names of the artists. "De Hooch," he whispered, "De Hooch. Hondecoeter."

He thought the name Hondecoeter was the most exciting name he had ever heard. He would call himself Hondecoeter if he ever had to change his name. He had heard that in Scotland you could call yourself whatever you wanted. He would choose Hondecoeter.

4

Those summers in Argyll, so long when you looked at them on the calendar, seemed to her to pass far too quickly.

They did not see one another between the end of September and the middle of June. She wrote to him and sent him a Christmas card each year, but he did not reply.

"It's very rude," she said reproachfully. "If somebody writes you a letter, then you should write back. That's the rule, you know."

They were sixteen now, and July had drawn a mantle of warm air over Scotland. The hills of Skye were shimmering and blue, the sea glassy smooth and reflective.

"Even if you've got nothing to say?"

She laughed. "Yes, even if you've got nothing to say. You write back to the person and say *Thank you for your letter. I regret to say that nothing has happened to me, but I really enjoyed reading your letter. Please write again soon.* And then you finish off with *Yours sincerely*, followed by your name." She paused. "If you're writing to a friend, you can say *Love from* and then sign your name after that."

She looked at him. She knew that her words would have no effect. He ignored her; he always did. He looked straight ahead when she spoke to him, as if seeing something else altogether. It was most annoying, but she knew that if she revealed how irritating it was he would simply look straight ahead while she told him off. She had read a story recently where a woman kept closing her eyes and saying to herself *Men!* She felt like doing that now. *Men!*

"Besides," she continued, "you can't really say that nothing has happened to you. I know that you have plenty of things happening to you. Things happen at school don't they? They must do."

He shrugged. "Not a lot."

"I don't believe that. You put a whole lot of boys in a school, and things will happen. There'll be fights, won't there? Boys fight a lot. You could tell me about that. You play sports, don't you? Isn't there rugby there? What about fencing? Are you allowed to do fencing? And the food? Don't tell me they don't feed you—you could write to me and tell me what they give you to eat. I'm interested in all these things, you know."

"The food's horrible," he said. "They say that the cooks spit in the stew. All of them. They have spitting competitions in the kitchen."

"Well, there you are," she said, a note of triumph in her voice. "You could have written to me and told me about the cooks spitting in the stew."

He shook his head. "I've never seen it myself. I can't be sure it happens."

"Well, you could have said that you weren't sure. I'd still be interested to read about things that might have happened."

He lapsed into silence. She watched him. She liked doing that, simply watching him, even if he was ignoring her. Sometimes he would sit there with that sketchbook of his, completely absorbed, and draw while she watched him.

"You could do me," she said. "If you wanted to draw me, I'd say yes, you know."

He continued with his sketch of a dove that he had found lying underneath a tree, undamaged but dead. He had stretched out the wing and was drawing the feathers. He thought of how it was such a waste for nature to make something like this, a creature so intricate, and then for it to die beneath the tree that was its home, just like that.

"If you drew me," she said, "then you could give the picture to my mother. Or I could even buy it. I'll give you two shillings for it—maybe a bit more if you get a good likeness."

"I'll think about it," he said. "I'm drawing a dove at the moment."

She wished that he would pay more attention to her. Since he had gone to that school, something seemed to have happened. Of course he still spent time with her—most days they were together, although she remarked that she always had to come over to see him as he never made the journey to her house.

"You could ride over on your bike," she said. "It's not all that far, especially on a bicycle. Or you could even walk. I walk over every day, you know. It only takes me forty-five minutes. Or you could ask your father to drive you over in his car. You could do that, you know."

"Maybe."

She sighed. "We could go on a picnic tomorrow. I could make sandwiches for both of us. And some chicken. I could get some roast chicken legs. We could have them cold. And cake too. We've got lots of cake because my mother likes baking and we can't eat it all."

"Maybe."

Her frustration showed. "Don't just say maybe. What if the Prime Minister said maybe to everything? What if they brought some new law for him to sign and he just said *maybe?*"

"That's not how it works. He has somebody to sign for him. He can't sit there all the time signing papers. He's got plenty of other things to do."

She shook her head. "You're very wrong, Harry. You're

wrong about that—and a whole lot of other things. You still get things wrong."

He was silent for a while. Then he said, "Do you think there really are angels? Do you think they have wings like this?"

He held out the dove's wing, spreading the feathers.

"I'm not sure about angels," she said. "I don't think they really exist. People talk about them, but if they existed, then surely we would have seen them."

"Or they would have found feathers," he said. "We find eagle feathers, you know. Mr. Thompson found one the other day."

She had been confirmed in the Episcopal Church of Scotland, at her mother's instance; her father had no time for bishops. There had been talk of saints, but nothing had been said about angels, as she far as she could recall. "Yes, you would have thought that there would be feathers. But there aren't. So, no, I think angels are imaginary—like elves and fairies and so on. Only the weak-minded believe in such nonsense."

"And God?"

She caught her breath. "You shouldn't ask questions like that."

He busied himself with his sketchbook. "Surely we would have seen God by now. They've got those big telescopes. Surely we should have seen him."

"God is invisible," she announced. "You can't see him through a telescope."

"But if he's all powerful—and you know that hymn that says that? *Almighty, invisible God, la, la, la* . . . If he were so mighty, then he would be able to let people see him and then they'd behave better and we wouldn't have had the Great War, would we? God would have stopped it. God would have stopped all those men killing one another. He would have deflected the bullet that went into your father's leg . . ."

He stopped himself. She was glaring at him. "I don't know about that. And I don't want to know. My father's leg has nothing to do with it and I don't think you should talk about it in that way. He, at least, was in the trenches . . ." Now it was her turn to feel that she had crossed some invisible line; her mother had told her it was tactless to talk about who went and who stayed behind. "Anyway. I've got enough to think of, Harry—you may not have anything to think about, but I've got plenty."

She rose to her feet. "We'll have a picnic tomorrow, right? Up by the waterfall?"

He agreed. He had finished the sketch of the dove and he showed it to her.

The potentially awkward direction of the theological conversation was forgotten. She studied the shape of the pinions, traced with a transcendent delicacy. "You're going to be really famous, Harry," she said.

"Oh, I don't know . . ."

"Yes, you are. You're going to be very famous and I'm going to help you. You know that, don't you? You're going to be an artist of great distinction." She liked the sound of the phrase, and repeated it. "An artist of great distinction."

He said nothing. He never thought about his own future, which was something that would happen, of course, but could not be guessed at. She, it seemed, was the one who thought about him, who had ideas as to what he would do.

He carried the picnic basket—a hamper with a handle of desiccated leather. He walked ahead, up the rough path that led to the point where the burn tumbled off the lip of a hanging valley, creating a waterfall of thirty feet, a few wisps of white in dry weather but now, after the previous night's rain, a convincing torrent. At the foot of the waterfall was a pool, hollowed out of rock, in which the water lingered before completing its short journey to the sea.

He put the hamper down on the flat rock beside the water.

"I want to climb up to the top," he said, pointing to the head of the waterfall.

"Be careful," she said. "Wet rock is slippery."

He began to clamber up the rocks. Once at the top he looked down through the spray that the wind blew up in thin white puffs, like smoke, he thought. He saw that she was looking up at him, and he waved. He felt light-headed.

He made his way back down to the pool. He felt warm, not just because of the exertion of the climb, but because the sun was high in a cloudless sky. It was noon.

She had opened the hamper and extracted two plates on which she laid out the chicken and the sandwiches. There was a bottle of lemonade, still cool, from which she had poured a glass for him and one for her.

"Lemonade makes me sneeze," he said.

"It's the bubbles."

"They get up my nose."

She laughed. "Hold your nose while you drink."

He tried, but the lemonade ran down the front of his shirt. "Look what you've made me do."

She took a napkin from the hamper, soaking it from an upended bottle of water, and then dabbing at the moist patch on the shirt. "Take it off," she said. "It'll dry on the rock."

The moisture felt uncomfortable against his skin, and he did as she told him to do. She watched him, but when she saw that he noticed her, she looked away.

"Here," he said, passing the shirt to her.

He sat down, his arms hugging his knees. "It's so hot," he said.

She laid the shirt out on the rock. "We could swim," she said. "The water will cool us off."

He said nothing.

"Why not?" she said.

"Why not what?"

"Why not swim?"

He bit his lip. His heart was racing; he felt it. He was warmer than he had been before. "I haven't brought my swimming trunks. I didn't think it would be so hot."

"That doesn't matter."

His heart hammered within him. "But we can't swim if we haven't . . ."

She leaned over. She put a finger against his lips. "There's nobody to see us."

She stood up and he saw that she was beginning to undo her blouse. He stared down at the rock. He was at a boarding school and was used to nudity, but not this.

"What if somebody comes?" he said.

"They won't," she said. "Come on."

He stood up and began to unbuckle his belt. He turned, so that his back was to her, and soon he was naked. He did not look at her. He looked only at the sky and the water.

There was a splash. She had jumped into the water, and was calling him from the pool. He kept his eyes on the sky, not looking where he was going. He felt the breath of the wind on his skin and then the cool embrace of the water.

She was beside him. He looked at her and smiled. Her hair was bedraggled. He felt her touch him—her foot had kicked against his inadvertently. The water was shallow and he leaned back, the rock beneath him.

She said, "I feel that I've known you for ever."

"Well, you have, I suppose."

She had moved closer to him. "Are you cold?"

"No," he said.

"Neither am I. When you first get in, you feel cold, but then it goes, doesn't it?"

"Yes."

That was in late July. By mid-September he was back at school, more senior now in the hierarchy, eligible for the few highly sought-after privileges given to those in their last two years there. He had a study to share with another boy, and he used his half of this as a studio. A sympathetic art master had spotted his talent and was encouraging him. "I see you at the art college in Edinburgh," the teacher said. "My own alma mater, of course, and I would hesitate to influence you too much but . . . well, we had the most marvellous fun there, you know. And at the same time we received a very fine education in drawing and painting—every bit as good as what you'd find in Florence."

He needed no persuading. "That's what I want," he said.

"Well then, you know what to do . . . draw, draw, draw. Have your sketchbook with you at all times. Look at the world and see the lines. The world is all lines, you know—lines and shapes. See them; feel them, Harry. Lines and shapes."

He was drawing when word came that his housemaster wanted to see him.

"Trouble," said the boy who came to fetch him. "You know how he looks when he's angry? Well, sorry to say, that's how he looks. But double it."

He searched his memory. "I've done nothing . . ."

The other boy shrugged. "I'm only saying what I saw."

He knocked at the door and was called in. His father was there, sitting in a chair by the housemaster's desk.

His heart stopped. His mother had died. That was the only explanation for his father's presence.

"Sit down," said the housemaster flatly before turning to Harry's father. "Mr. MacGregor?"

His father looked at him but only held his gaze for a few moments before looking away. "Do you realise what you've done?" he said, his voice strained with emotion. "Do you have the faintest idea?"

Harry felt perplexed. He did not know what to say. And then he realised this could be only one thing. Somebody had seen them.

"Because if you don't," his father continued, "I'm going to have to spell it out to you."

The boy started to shake. He was unprepared for it, but it took hold of him, starting in his hands. He grasped them together, hoping to stop the movement.

"You have made that girl pregnant," said his father. "You . . . yes, you have done that."

He closed his eyes. It had simply not occurred to him, possibly because he had blocked it out. The guilt—and there had been guilt—had obscured the more practical issue.

He spoke automatically. "I didn't."

His father stood up, towering above him. His face bore an expression he had not seen before—one of pure anger. "Don't deny it, Harry. Don't add lies to your mountain of misdeeds."

The housemaster raised a hand. "Mr. MacGregor, perhaps . . ."

"I'm sorry," said his father. "I shall try to control myself."

"Your feelings are completely understandable," said the housemaster quietly.

They both looked at Harry.

"We have made every effort to contain the situation," said his father. "I have spoken at length to her father, who has been extremely understanding—more so, in fact, than one could reasonably hope for in normal circumstances. That, at least, has made our position less awkward."

The housemaster nodded. "That's fortunate," he said.

"Jenny has been sent down south. There's a place where girls who . . . girls who get themselves into trouble are able to go and have the baby. They arrange adoption."

The baby. He caught his breath. This was about a *baby*. This was not about something that happened on that picnic, with the waterfall behind them and the sun. The full enormity of what he had done came home to him. He started to cry.

"I'm going to kill myself," he said.

The words came unbidden, and their effect was immediate. His father gasped, and exchanged a quick glance with the housemaster.

"Don't say things like that," said the housemaster. "You don't mean that, Harry."

"I do." He felt his body shaking with his sobs. He wanted to die.

His father moved over towards him. He put his arm around his shoulder. "Listen, Harry, this is not a tragedy. This is a mistake that . . . well, that happens. We had to talk to you about it. We had to make sure that you understood."

The housemaster rose from his desk and crossed the room. A boy had committed suicide the previous year—

a boy under his care. That had been something to do with sex as well. You had to be so careful with these young people. They were impetuous.

"We think that perhaps it would be best if you went home, Harry," said the housemaster. "I think what you've just said is not something you really mean. Go home with your father."

He struggled with his tears. "I'm to take all my things?"

The housemaster inclined his head. "Yes. I'm sorry about this, but we cannot countenance such things."

"You're not being expelled," said his father. "Mr. Sanderson—and the headmaster—have been very understanding. You're not even being asked to leave. You're going of your own accord."

"Yes," said the housemaster. "I don't for one moment approve of what you have done, and you will have time to reflect on that, I imagine. But I don't want to ruin your prospects. You're planning to go to art college, aren't you? I'm sure there'll be no difficulty with that. And I'm sure, too, that you will not repeat what you've done, will you?"

His father answered for him. "He will not. He won't be seeing the girl again. You can rest assured of that."

"Good," said the housemaster.

He offered Harry his hand to shake.

5

He took readily to the regime at the art college. They started early, even in the winter term, when the light that flooded through the windows of the great studios was a cold northern one, struggling to make an impression on the half-darkness in which winter clothed Scotland. There was little time for individual flourish—just the constant discipline of drawing under the critical eye of the tutors; they were artists themselves, some rumoured to lead a bohemian existence, but not here, not in the college with its formalities and proprieties.

He discovered the work of James Cowie, and made the trip to Hospitalfield to visit him. The quiet painter spoke to him about preparatory studies. "Do everything three, four times. And then do it again." He looked at the work that Harry had brought to show him, paging through the sketchbooks. "On the right lines," he said.

In 1939, shortly after his nineteenth birthday, he went to Glasgow to visit Fergusson, who had returned to Scotland from France. "Painting under a cloud is going to be difficult," Fergusson said to him. "The light will be blocked out, you know. That's what's happening now in Europe—the light is being blocked out."

On the train back to Edinburgh, he sat in his compartment with a kilted soldier, a corporal. The man said nothing, but as the train drew into the station, he lowered the window, opened the door, and leapt out onto the platform. Harry struggled with the swinging door but managed to close it before the train came to a halt. He sketched the incident in his sketchbook—the man's back, the pleats of the kilt caught in the wind, the Edinburgh skyline in the distance.

Later, sitting at the table in his lodgings with the young man with whom he shared a room, a medical student, he described what happened. "Despair," said the medical student. "We see it in the infirmary every day—or almost every day. Despair. Guilt."

He asked him about guilt. "Why do we feel guilty?"

The medical student laughed. "Because there are plenty of people who are only too ready to peddle guilt. The Wee

Free Church does it. They're always at each others' throats, but they're made of the same hodden, you know. And they find fertile ground for their efforts, believe me." He paused, looking at his watch. Their landlady was slow; even the cooking of a haddock seemed to take her for ever. "Your problem, Harry, is that you will never have done anything that makes you feel that way."

He looked at him. "How can you tell?"

The medical student laughed. "Because if you had, I could see it in your eyes."

Harry held his gaze.

"I believe I might see something," said the medical student. "What is it, old fellow? Something to confess?"

"No."

"That tells me everything. People who say they have nothing to confess have everything to confess."

In a dream that night he saw his baby. It came to him and stretched out a hand. It was wearing white, a *mort claith,* he thought, the Scots term for a shroud. It tried to say something to him, but was taken away by a woman in a blue tunic. And suddenly the child was no longer there, but had been replaced by a man in a grey suit who said, "Draw everything twice, Mr. MacGregor."

. . .

In 1940, at the age of twenty, he left the art college and enlisted in the Argyll and Sutherland Highlanders. "You're doing the right thing," said the college principal. "Your place will be open when hostilities are over." It was shortly after Dunkirk, and he had none of the illusions of the previous year.

"You'll be an officer, I take it," said the principal.

He shrugged.

"But of course you will be. Were you in the Corps at school? Yes? Because that's what they look at."

"I'm not sure that I'm cut out for that."

"For leadership? But of course you are. Listen, one of the things we do here is instil self-discipline. Drawing class at eight thirty in the morning is exactly the sort of thing that develops that . . . that ability to cope with the world. The average young man won't have that, you know."

"Miners start early . . ."

"That's not the point. Miners are not officer material."

The principal was right. He was sent off on a week's selection course and emerged an officer cadet. Four months later he was commissioned, and found himself in charge of a platoon of men recruited from rural Argyll. Some of them seemed to be no more than boys—sixteen-year-olds taken from the farms where they were starting their lives as stockmen, shepherds, gamekeepers. They looked at him as if he came from another world, accepting an authority that for his part he felt he had no right to exercise.

He was sent to North Africa. In 1942, he was at El Alamein. He had been seconded to a camouflage unit, and his skill at creating the illusion of tanks and fuel dumps out of netting and wood had been noticed by his superiors. He was promoted to captain and mentioned in despatches. He saw Monty himself, who inspected one of his bogus tanks and pronounced it good. "I'm not fooled, of course," he said. "But let's hope that General Rommel is."

A few days after the victory, he was in Cairo. In Shepheard's Hotel a man in the uniform of a lieutenant in the Royal Scots Greys came up and introduced himself. The lieutenant offered to buy him a drink. "I feel I almost know you," he said. "But not quite. My cousin, you see, is Jenny Currie—you two were quite friendly, I believe."

When the other man returned from the bar, Harry's hand trembled as he took the drink. They exchanged toasts.

"Somebody said that you were up at El Alamein," said the lieutenant. "Well done. I hear you were one of the camouflage chaps. Magicians, people said. You made things disappear."

"They remained exactly where they were," he said. "We just made it look as if they were something they weren't. The human eye will believe what it wants to see."

"Oh, I know that," said the lieutenant. "Try looking out of a tank in the desert."

They had lapsed into silence before he summoned up his courage. "What news of Jenny, then?"

The cousin visibly relaxed. "I thought you were never going to ask." He paused. "You see, I do know about . . ." He left the sentence unfinished.

Harry felt himself blushing, and the younger man noticed it.

"I'm sorry. Perhaps I shouldn't have mentioned it."

He reached out and laid a hand on the other man's forearm. The cousin looked down with surprise at the hand on his arm. Harry withdrew it.

"No, I'm glad you did. I'm very ashamed, you see . . ." He broke off.

The cousin lowered his voice. "Don't be embarrassed," he said. "Look, both of us have seen enough in the last two months to teach us not to be awkward about things. Enough death, I mean. I've had my men roasted before my eyes, their tanks an oven. My God, if you've seen that, then you're not going to worry about something like this. A small thing. A very small thing."

He felt his eyes begin to fill with tears. *I can't cry. Not here, in Shepheard's Hotel. I can't cry.*

The cousin saw what was happening. "Look, she's fine. She's absolutely fine. She had the baby . . ."

"What was it?"

The cousin smiled. "It was a girl."

He almost asked about the adoption, but thought there was no point. "And Jenny herself?"

"You didn't hear about her marriage?"

He felt himself reeling. "I was forbidden to try to contact her. Her father and mine agreed. I was not to see her."

The cousin managed a weak smile. "I think she knew that. I don't think she thought you were deliberately cold-shouldering her. She was told the same thing, I understand. Her mother came down on her like a ton of bricks. You were to be off-limits."

He wanted to know about the marriage.

"A fellow from Glasgow," said the cousin. "They're a ship-building family. He's a naval architect and so they've left him where he is. They've recently built a corvette. I saw pictures of the launch. They're doing well, of course, with the need for shipping."

He nodded.

The cousin continued. "He's a perfectly decent type. He's a bit older than she is—thirty-five, thirty-six."

"And children? Do they have children?"

"None since . . ." He tailed off.

Harry looked down at his drink. "Are you in touch with her?"

"Yes, of course. I haven't seen her for a long time, of course, but I had a letter the other day. We occasionally write to one another. In fact, she was the one who told me that I might bump into you. I don't know where she'd heard you were here, but she seemed to know."

Harry hesitated. "Will you pass on a message from me?"

A shadow passed over the cousin's face. "She's happily married, you know . . ."

"Of course, of course."

"So I'm not sure that you should write to her."

"Which is precisely why I'm asking you to pass on a message."

"Yes, all right."

But now he was unsure what to say. He heard the words of the song, the words that everyone knew. *Will you please say hello to the folks that I know . . . They'll be happy to know that as you saw me go, I was singing this song . . .*

People took comfort in that; in the folksy optimism of it. But he did not want to pass on a cliché. So he said, "Tell her that I'm terribly sorry."

The cousin inclined his head. "I'll write to her," he said. "I'll say that." He paused. "We all have something to be sorry about. Every one of us. And we often don't have the chance to say anything about it because we're . . . because we're ashamed. Then it's too late. Your tank gets it. You tread on a mine. A sniper lines you up in his sights, and it's too late."

"Oh well . . ."

The cousin seemed to want to continue. There were many conversations like this in wartime, thought Harry. Things that had not been said, were said; people felt liberated, released from their normal inhibitions, by the possibility of imminent death.

"It's not a girl with me," said the cousin. "It's a boy."

Harry said nothing.

"And now it's too late."

"The War?"

"Yes."

Harry met his eyes. "I'm very sorry."

"Thank you. Nobody knows."

"I can understand that," said Harry. "But you don't have to worry about telling me."

"You're an artist . . ."

"Exactly. And anyway, I've felt the same thing myself, on occasion. So you're not alone. You may think you are, but that's just because others are afraid of honesty."

"But . . ."

"But there are all sorts of possibilities. Love can occur in so many different ways, if we let it. Nothing is as clear-cut as people would like to think it is."

6

For some years after the War he painted very little. He took a job teaching art in a school; it was unchallenging, but he found that he enjoyed it rather more than he had anticipated. He drifted into a relationship with a woman who taught history at the same school, and they lived together for almost ten years, before they parted, without acrimony and slightly regretfully. After his father died, he decided to sell the house in Argyll. He had spent very little time there, anyway—no more than a few weeks every summer. He went back to the waterfall, though, every visit, and on each occasion he found himself moved by the experience. The places that loom large in our lives, the places where things have happened that we cannot forget, can retain their power over us for as long as memory persists. Here I was sad; here I saw you for the last time; here I realised I was in love: these private thoughts can be attached to a place, as inseparable from it in our minds as its prevailing weather.

The history teacher said to him, "You're in love with somebody else, you know. Who is she? Can't you tell me?"

He frowned. "I wouldn't deceive you."

"Oh, I'm not talking about that. I'm not accusing you of having another lover—not right now, not somebody you're seeing."

He somehow knew that her words signalled the end of their affair. Ten years could be brought to an end with a few words of reproach, or, as in this case, of truth. But he did not want to admit it. "Then what are you saying?"

"I'm saying that there's somebody you've never got over—somebody you're never going to forget."

He had been silent.

"I'm right, aren't I?" she said.

He did not answer.

She sighed. "There are some people who hold a candle for somebody else—a first love, perhaps. They hold it all their lives, in some cases until they die." She looked away. "Don't you think that sad?"

He nodded.

There was no recrimination in her tone. "To spend your life with the wrong person . . . That must be a terrible thing, you know. You're with one person and you want to be with another. And you know that we only have one shot at life, one chance, and that you've wasted yours."

A month after this conversation, they went their separate ways. With the sale of the estate, he was able to resign from the school and return to painting. He surprised himself. He had not imagined that there was so much that he wanted to say and that it could come so urgently, so effortlessly. He submitted a painting to an open competition, and it was not only accepted for display, but won an award. A friend urged him to work for a show. There was an exhibition in Edinburgh and one, for his fortieth birthday, in London.

He was taken on by an influential gallery and his paintings were bought by collectors. He attracted press attention; being described in one review as a successor to Nash and Ravilious. Another said he was a neo-classical answer to the excesses of modernism, an afterthought to a movement that was far from finished. His friends found this amusing. "How does it feel to be an afterthought?"

"Strange. Not entirely unsatisfactory."

"Like a footnote to history?"

He laughed. "A bit like that, perhaps."

He drafted a letter to Jenny. He said, "I know that I shouldn't be writing to you. I know that you are married now and that everything that happened between us is a long time ago. I know all that, but I still didn't want to die—as we all must—I didn't want to go to my grave without telling you that I wish that things had turned out differently. I have had a lifetime to regret what happened and what didn't happen. That's all I want so say."

He read what he had written. He tore the letter up, oddly aware, even as he did so, that he was making a further mistake to add to those that had gone before.

As his reputation as a painter grew, he attracted the

attention of wealthy patrons. Berenson invited him to I Tatti and suggested a lecture in Florence. "I have little to say," he remarked. "I draw."

"And how!" said Berenson.

While at I Tatti he was invited to lunch by a woman from Pittsburgh, the wife of a steel manufacturer. She had a villa in the hills near Fiesole and she gave lunch parties that were often mentioned in the press. Her salon hosted Blunt, Auden and Britten, as well as Hemingway, whom she was said not to like.

He went to the lunch, at which there were over twenty guests. They were served what was described as a simple Tuscan lunch, but which ran to six courses. Just before they sat down, the last of the guests arrived.

He saw that it was Jenny.

He manoeuvred himself away from the seat he was about to take. Leaning down, he whispered into the ear of the man who was to be seated next to Jenny. "Would you mind terribly? We're very old friends . . ."

The man looked up at him resentfully and was about to refuse when Jenny leaned over too. "Please," she said. "It's very important."

The other guest agreed, but with very bad grace.

"What a horrible man," Jenny whispered.

"People are selfish," he whispered back.

Then they looked at one another. It was 1968, and they were both coming up for their forty-eighth birthday. They had not seen one another for thirty-two years.

He said, "I don't know where to begin."

"I've followed your career," she said. "I know about most of it."

"You always did. You knew more about me, I thought, than I did myself."

She smiled. "I heard from Angus."

He looked blank.

"My cousin. He wrote to me just before he was killed."

"I didn't know . . ."

"He died in a stupid way. That happened to so many people. They survived those horrendous battles and then they fell down stairs or something like that. Angus choked on an olive."

"I'm sorry to hear that."

"He was a complex man. There was something that made him unhappy—I never worked it out." She paused. "Did you have any idea? Did you hear anything?"

He shook his head. *The dead may still wish their confidences to be respected.*

"He passed on my message?"

She reached for a glass of water. "He did. And you had nothing to apologise for, you know."

On the other side of the table another guest was holding forth, to the amusement of the general company. Harry and Jenny took it as cover.

He spoke with urgency, as if he might suddenly be silenced, and lose his chance to say what he had to say. "There hasn't been a day—not one single day—when I haven't thought of you. You know that? Not one day."

If she was surprised, she did not show it.

"And I've thought of your baby . . . our baby, and what it must have meant to you to go through with it all and then have the baby taken away from you."

She looked down at her hands. Then she raised her eyes. "But she wasn't," she said. "I kept the baby. We were discreet about it. My mother raised her for the first few years. Then I married when I was just twenty. I was very young, but remember it was wartime, and people did."

He struggled with the revelation. "You kept her?"

Jenny nodded. "Noel—he was my husband—was perfectly happy to be stepfather. He was a wonderful stepfather, by the way."

His mouth felt dry. "Was . . ."

"Noel died. He had a heart problem that nobody knew anything about. It was one of these hidden things. He died eight years ago." She took a sip of water. "His family had a villa in southern Tuscany. I started to use it more and more, and now I'm there most of the year. Julie comes often, even if only for a week or two. Her husband can't get away all that much. He's a psychiatrist."

He sat quite still.

"She's here at present. I've left her down at San Casciano with her two little ones."

"Julie . . ."

She looked at him. "Our daughter," she said.

He looked up at the painted ceiling. A line of cypress trees crossed a Tuscan hillside. Angels, della Robbia in appearance, crossed a clear blue sky.

It came back to him. "Do you remember that we once talked about angels? Do you remember that?"

She toyed with her fork. "I think I do."

He pointed to the ceiling. "There," he said. "Look up there."

It was while she was looking up that he said, "Do you think that you might marry me? After all this time?"

She did not answer immediately. After thirty-two years, she thought, what was a minute or two, even five?

Dear Ventriloquist

I

In any photograph of the land, there is the land and the person who takes the photograph. In any photograph of two people there are three people: the two in the picture, in this case the man sitting on the woman's lap, and then there is the person behind the camera. We see the two people, smiling over something, pleased that they are there rather than somewhere else, pleased, we assume, that they are who they are rather than being somebody else. We do not see the young man who has pressed the lever to open the shutter. We do not see that he is twenty-two, that his hair is cut short, that he is wearing working trousers, that when he has taken this photograph he steps forward and shakes the man's hand, and that the woman then stands up, dusts down her skirt, and says to him: "Thank you, Eddie."

Sometimes we can tell what the person behind the camera is thinking. Sometimes the choice of subject is so striking that it can only be the work of an attentive and sympathetic eye, attuned to the moment. In those famous photographs of men and women caught up in war—that poor girl running naked from the napalm, for instance—it is the photographer's understanding of what is happening, his feeling for the sorrow or terror of what he sees, that gives the photograph its impact, that makes it every bit as powerful as a painting by Titian, say, or Picasso's great indictment in *Guernica*.

Often we have no idea of who the photographer was, or what he was thinking at the time. He may have been a passer-by, asked to take a photograph with the subject's own camera; he may have been a professional photographer just doing a job, not caring very much about the people he is photographing; he may even have been one who would have wished for some reason to be in the photograph himself. What if Eddie, who took this photograph, secretly imagined that it was he, rather than Frank, who was sitting on Ruby's lap? A photograph may speak to the photographer's envy or disappointment just as much as it may reveal his anger or disapproval. And even if a photograph records a joyous occasion, behind it there may still be more than a small measure of heartbreak on the part of the photographer. A small measure of heartbreak? One might think such a thing impossible—if your heart is broken, then surely it is broken completely. Yet the truth is that we can live with a minor fault-line in the heart—most of us do, in one way or another.

. . .

Eddie, as the woman addressed him, was Edward Orpheus Beaulieu, who was born in Kingston, Ontario, on an unusually hot afternoon exactly seven months into the twentieth century. His mother, Hope, was from Toronto, a member of a family who owned a successful grocery store; his father, Aristide, had been a fur trapper in Quebec, but had grown tired of the loneliness and discomfort involved in trapping. Having taken a course in bookkeeping, he established a small office in Kingston and set about gathering clients. He discovered a talent for making up figures for traders who had been lax in keeping a note of money-in and money-out. He did this as honestly as he could, hoping that the entries he made reflected what had actually happened. If anything, he erred on the side of caution, with the result that many of his clients paid slightly more tax than they were required to pay, but, as he pointed out to any who objected, "At least you can sleep easily in your bed if you've paid the government too much."

Eddie was an only son, although he had two sisters, Martine and Joan, both of whom married early—Martine at seventeen and Joan at nineteen. Martine moved with her husband, a glazier, to Buffalo, New York, while Joan married a farmer from Guelph. The Beaulieu parents were proud of their two girls, and of the sound marriages they had made.

They were quickly rewarded with grandchildren, including a set of twins.

"Our girls know where they're going," confided Hope to a close friend. "Unfortunately, Eddie doesn't have quite the same sense of who he is and what he wants to be."

The friend sympathised. She did not know that Hope Beaulieu was completely wrong. Sometimes the reason why parents think their offspring have no idea of what they want to do is that they simply cannot accept their child's real wishes. Eddie knew exactly what he wanted to do: he wanted to be a showman, and, in particular, a fortune-teller.

This ambition showed itself at an early stage when, as a schoolboy of twelve, he was found to be reading palms in the school playground for two cents a time.

"You're going to be very rich," he would tell the boys. "You won't be rich until you're very old—probably about thirty—but then you'll be one of the richest men in Canada. It's here in the lines on your hand. See? That one there. You only have that shape of line if you're destined to be rich."

That went down very well. But there was more.

"You're going to marry a woman with very big breasts. See those bumps in your palm—right there—see those? That's the sign. You'll marry her—but only if you want. If you do, then you're going to have five sons, and all of them are going to be great hockey players—real champs. You're going to die when you are just short of one hundred. You'll have only four teeth left by then—two on the top and two on the bottom. But you're going to be real happy."

That was a typical fortune for a boy, although there were considerable variations, depending on whether Eddie liked or disliked the boy consulting him. Those whom he disliked were often warned of impending disaster, sometimes in fairly vivid terms. "Be careful that you don't go out in really cold weather," he might say. "This line here tells me that your nose is going to get frostbite one of these days—I can't tell when—but when it happens, you're going to lose half of it. Sorry about that, but I have to mention bad things as well as good."

Fortunes for girls tended to cater for more feminine interests. "You're going to marry a guy called Percy who has a big house in Toronto, with two maids. You'll marry this guy after you've received proposals from many other men. You'll reject them all because you only want to marry the one you love, who has this big house in Toronto."

The authorities discouraged him. "Edward Beaulieu," scolded his teacher, "if I catch you telling fortunes one more time you're going to get such a tanning that you won't sit down for a week. That's your future, young man. So heed what I say."

Even if this led to greater discretion, the interest in fortune-telling persisted, although as he progressed into the later teen years he also became adept in card tricks, conjuring, and Pelmanism. He discussed each new interest with his parents, demonstrating his tricks, lapping up their praise when one of the tricks worked. They were generally tolerant of their son, but, as the years passed and he showed no signs of leaving home, they began to find his company rather tiring.

"If only Eddie would think of . . . ," began his mother.

"Moving on?"

She looked at her husband. "It's not that I find him . . ."

"Tedious?"

She gave her husband another look. "Eddie could do so much for the world," she said.

He raised an eyebrow. "You sure, honey?"

"It's just a question of his finding what he really wants."

Eddie's father shrugged. "He seems to have quite a good idea already."

"But none of this stuff will earn him a living, Aristide.

He's got to get a proper job. He can't get by helping in that store four mornings a week. He can't live on that."

"Well, he seems to think he can," said his father.

She shook her head. "Because we don't charge him rent. If he had to pay rent, he wouldn't have enough to keep body and soul together. You're going to have to talk to him again, you know."

When it occurred, that conversation ended just as had the last one on the subject—in stalemate.

"Eddie," said his father, "I'm talking to you man-to-man. You're twenty now, which means you're not a boy any more. You're a man, and men have to get out there and work."

"I'm already working, Dad: Henderson's store. And Mr. Henderson said the other day that he couldn't imagine how he could run his store without me." He paused, watching the effect of his words. "That's what he said."

"That's as may be," said his father. "I know that you're not a slacker. It's just that that job is never going to be more than part-time. Old Henderson can't pay more than you get already."

"Something will turn up, Dad. I'm keeping an eye open. And I'm studying, remember?"

"This Pelmanism of yours?"

"Yes, that's it. I'm sticking with it, Dad, because it has the answer we're all looking for."

His father fixed him with a stare. "What *is* the answer then?"

Eddie sighed. It was hard to explain things to his parents. It was not that they were slow; it was more a question of getting through to them. They were on one wavelength and he was on another. That could happen, he knew, even when people lived in the same house, read the same newspaper, did much the same things in their everyday lives.

"I don't know the answer, Dad," he said. "That's what I'm trying to find out. That takes time."

"Well, what's the question? You don't know the answer, but then what's the question you're trying to answer? Maybe you can explain it that way. Who knows?"

There was another patient sigh. "The question is . . . Well, I'm trying to find out what the question is. That takes time too—and a lot of study."

"So you don't know the question and you don't know the answer. That means you don't know nothing, doesn't it?"

"You don't say *you don't know nothing,* Dad. I know it's difficult for you—being French and all—but you don't say *don't know nothing*. Not in English. That means you know something, because nothing is the opposite of something, and if you don't know nothing you must know something."

Now it was his father's turn to sigh—a deep, heartfelt sigh, followed by a gazing up at the ceiling, as if to find there the elusive answer to the equally elusive question.

2

Hope persuaded him to apply for a job with the postal service. He was interviewed in Kingston, and she accompanied him to his appointment, sitting in the waiting room while he went inside. She had only ten minutes to wait before he came out, picked up his hat, and walked out on to the street without giving her a glance.

The chairman of the interview panel emerged and looked at her anxiously. She knew him from the church they both attended. He held out his hands in a gesture of resignation and, she thought, apology.

"I'm very sorry, Mrs. Beaulieu."

She bit her lip. "It didn't go well?"

"I did my best, but he didn't really answer the questions the board asked him."

"He refused? He refused to speak?"

The chairman shook his head. "No, it was the opposite problem, really. He spoke rather too much, but about the wrong things. He went on about this . . . this . . ."

"Pelmanism?"

There was flicker of a smile on the chairman's lips. "Yes, that's it. He seemed to think it relevant to our questions, but frankly it wasn't. So we more or less dried up, I'm afraid."

She shook her head. "I'm very sorry, Mr. Andrews. You know how young people are these days—they get ideas. He's a good boy, Eddie, and he's a hard worker, you know. He's never been afraid of hard work."

"I'm sure. Bobby Henderson speaks highly of him—always has."

"It's just that he has these odd interests. He loves telling fortunes; card tricks too. And this Pelmanism . . . it's a sort of hocus-pocus memory course as far as I can make out."

The chairman looked at his hands. "He'll find something. I always say to my boys that whatever shape of peg you are, there's a hole for you somewhere." He paused. He knew that was only partly true, and an aphorism that was only partly true was hardly an aphorism at all.

She walked home and told her husband what had happened. He rose from his desk and walked to the window. His breathing was shallow—a sign of the anger that was welling up within him. Why couldn't Eddie be like his sisters? Where did he *come from*? Why did he feel that he had to spend the evening—every evening—practising his conjuring tricks on them, making them listen to his endless lectures on Pelmanism? How many times had he himself fled the house on the pretext of having work to do in the office, leaving his wife to bear the brunt? "I'm going to give him an ultimatum. I'm going to tell him we have to start charging him rent."

"But he can't pay much."

"Then we tell him he's going to have to go."

She drew in her breath. She was as frustrated as her husband was, but she was a mother. "No, Aristide, we can't tell Eddie to go. He's our flesh and blood. You can't tell your own flesh and blood to go. You just can't."

He was silent for a few moments, but then his anger subsided; he had never been able to sustain it. "No, I don't suppose we can," he muttered. "But I'm going to start looking for a job for him—seriously. There must be something."

"Perhaps he could go into show business," said his wife. "He's a good conjurer—a very good one, some say. Remember what Mrs. Harper said when he pulled that mouse out of her purse. She was adamant there had been no mouse there before—adamant."

"Hmm. It's the sort of thing somebody might deny, of course."

"What? Having a mouse in your purse?"

He smiled. "Possibly."

She brought the conversation back to Eddie's talents. "And there are those card tricks of his. He could get a job in the theatre."

He thought about this. He remembered that one of his clients had a brother-in-law who was the proprietor of a small circus. He recalled his client saying to him a few days ago that his brother-in-law was staying with him because he had had an operation and needed somewhere quiet to spend a month while he recuperated. "He has a circus business," the client said. "Odd business, in my view, but he does pretty well out of it. He has a set-up in Toronto that tours over the border—Niagara and so on—as well as one over in Vancouver. He's making good money, you know."

"That's good."

"Yes. People love the circus, although I wouldn't fancy

living away from home—all that travelling and so on. No, not for me."

Nor for me, thought Mr. Beaulieu, but possibly for Eddie. In fact, what better job was there for a young man who needed encouragement to leave the nest?

"Have you ever thought of joining the circus, son?" he asked that evening.

The question was casually put, but it elicited an immediate response.

"Oh, that would be great—really great. I'd *love* a job in a circus."

"Would you now?" said Mr. Beaulieu, thoughtfully.

3

It proved simpler than Mr. Beaulieu had imagined. The owner of the Great All-Canada Circus was Mr. Gregory Paul Vink, a stout, rather dyspeptic-looking New Englander. Vink had married a Canadian nurse, the sister of Mr. Beaulieu's client, and had moved to Ontario to help her ageing parents on their farm. He was no farmer, and he soon looked around for something else to do. He had bought the circus from its previous owner after he had lost interest in it. The purchase price had been tiny, but so had the audiences at the time, as the circus had very little to offer, most of the performers having long since abandoned it on the grounds of non-payment of wages. Vink changed all that. He used what little capital he had to buy a new big tent and to offer advance payment to a number of artists. These he chose well, as he had an eye for showmanship, and before long the circus had acquired a reputation not only in Toronto, but in a number of other cities to which it toured: Winnipeg, Saskatoon, Calgary. This led to the acquisition of another circus, this one based in New Westminster, at the western end of the railway line spanning the country. He ran the two as a single business, in spite of the vast sea of land that lay between them, exchanging performers to keep everybody's act fresh.

"Nothing like a different audience to keep you on your toes," he observed.

When Mr. Beaulieu went to see him at his client's house, Vink was pleased to have a visitor.

"Sitting here all day," he said, "makes me itchy. The doc says I have to do it—they removed half my stomach, you know—but it drives me up the wall doing nothing here. It's nice to have some intelligent company for a change—not that my brother-in-law isn't intelligent, I hasten to point out."

"I've come about my boy," said Mr. Beaulieu. "I have a son of twenty, you see, and he's very keen to join a circus."

Mr. Beaulieu had not expected a laugh.

"Twenty?" chuckled Vink. "Usually it's ten-year-olds. I get letters every week. Kids have some row with their parents and so what happens? They write off to see if they can join the circus. It's what they do." He shook his head. "Little devils."

"He's very good at card tricks," said Mr. Beaulieu. "He's also a conjuror. He's been praised for that, I'm told. There was a theatrical group passed through town six months ago—big variety act. And one of them said he had a future on the stage."

"The circus ain't the theatre," said Vink. "If you want to go on the stage you go to New York. Or maybe Toronto."

"It's not theatre he wants," said Mr. Beaulieu. "It's the circus."

Vink looked thoughtful. "I might be able to interview him—see what he's like."

Mr. Beaulieu knew the dangers of that. If Eddie were to be interviewed, Vink would be treated to a discourse on Pelmanism or the uses of the Tarot pack. He would be rejected out of hand.

He had come prepared. "I have a proposition to make," he said. "I want to get my boy started . . ."

Vink interrupted him. "Oh, I understand that, Mr. Bowl . . ."

"Beaulieu."

"Mr. Beaulieu . . . I understand that."

"Thank you. I fully appreciate how tight things are in any business. So why don't we do this: I'll pay you his wages for the first three months. I'll wire you the money and you can pay him, so that he thinks it's coming from you. Then, after three months, you decide whether you're going to keep him."

"And if I like him, then I only start paying from the end of three months?"

"Yes, but until then there's no risk for you. You needn't put up a dime until that point. The risk lies with me."

Vink looked at him suspiciously. "What's wrong with this boy of yours?" he asked.

Mr. Beaulieu grinned nervously. "Why do you ask?"

"Because of the terms you're offering."

He made a quick decision. Vink was clearly astute, and

he would spot concealment. "He can go on a bit. He's a nice young man, but he goes on a bit."

Vink laughed. "Is that all? I thought maybe he was on the run or something like that. Wanted by the RCMP maybe."

"Oh no. He's one hundred per cent honest." He said this with a conviction that showed.

"In that case," said Vink, "I'll take him. I need a couple of new hands. We'll see how he shapes up."

"You won't regret it," said Mr. Beaulieu.

"Time will tell," said Vink. "It tells most things if you give it the chance."

"You're right there, Mr. Vink. *Time like an ever-rolling stream . . .*"

Vink took the reference. "*Bears all its sons away* . . . Oh, those old hymns have it, don't they, Mr. Beaulieu?"

"They sure do, Mr. Vink."

They shook hands, and Vink went back to his operation and to the length of the section of intestine that had been removed. "Two feet," he said. "Surgeon showed it to me afterwards."

"A circus, Dad? Toronto?"

Mr. Beaulieu smiled at his son. "Actually, he said that

he'd want you to start over in BC. They have a branch over there—place called New Westminster, just outside Vancouver. It's where the railway line ends."

"Oh, I know all about New Westminster," said Eddie, enthusiastically. "I've read about it. The Fraser River."

"He said you could start straight away. He'll give you the money for your railway ticket. Three days from Toronto, isn't it? All the way across."

"I'll make food for the journey," said Mrs. Beaulieu. "You won't go hungry."

"They have food on the train," said Eddie. "I've seen pictures of folks eating as they go across the prairies . . . eating at tables like they were at home but they're actually on the prairies, you see . . ."

"Yes, yes," said Mr. Beaulieu.

Eddie's smile faded. "It's a long way away, BC. Are you going to be all right back here? By yourselves?"

His parents exchanged a glance. "Eddie, you don't worry about us. You just seize this opportunity with both hands. Seize the day, as they say."

"You sure, Dad?"

"I'm one hundred per cent sure, Eddie. This is your big

chance." He feigned a playful punch at his son's shoulder. "Work hard and justify the faith Mr. Vink has in you. Work hard and you get to the top."

"The big top," said Eddie. "That's what they call a circus tent. The big top, eh, Dad?"

They laughed. "Good for you, son," said Mr. Beaulieu. "Your future is just beginning."

4

In New Westminster he was given lodgings in a boarding house two blocks away from the circus warehouse. Two young port workers lived there too, and the three of them were looked after by an indulgent landlady who referred to "her boys" and who not only cooked for them but also took it upon herself to launder and repair their clothes.

On his first day at work, he was taken round by the circus manager and introduced to all twenty-three people who ran the circus, from the men who erected the tent to the trapeze artists, a couple of Russian exiles, morose chain smokers who, when not practising or performing, sat in their trailer and wrote letters to their friends in Paris. They spoke virtually no English, but pretended to understand what was said to them, nodding in agreement until they could return to their lengthy correspondence.

"Your job," said the manager, "is going to be collecting tickets at the entrance, showing people to their seats, and cleaning up after each show. You're also going to be assistant to Frank—my second-in-command. You do whatever Frank wants you to do."

Eddie hid his disappointment. He had seen himself performing, even if he had yet to work out exactly what he could do. It was difficult to do card tricks in front of a large audience, but he could do some conjuring. He could make things disappear—it was simple enough—and people loved watching that.

The manager picked up this disappointment. "You got a problem with any of that?"

Eddie decided to take a risk. "Mr. Vink promised I could put on an act."

The manager frowned. "He didn't tell me nothing about that."

"Anything," said Eddie. "He didn't tell you anything about it. If he didn't tell you nothing, then he told you something."

The manager stroked the side of his neck. "What can you do?"

Eddie pointed to a small Jack Russell terrier sitting nearby. "That dog," he said.

"That's the human cannonball's dog. Jack—you'll meet him. Jack's mighty fond of that dog."

"I can make him disappear," said Eddie. "You want to see?"

"What do you need?"

Eddie pointed to a stack of small empty crates nearby. "Those boxes—can I use those?"

The manager nodded. "You make the dog disappear then. I'm watching."

Eddie arranged the boxes in a circle. Then he fetched the dog, who seemed not to object to having an upended crate put over him. From within a few barks could be heard—then silence.

"Right," said Eddie. "Tell me which box the dog is in."

The manager snorted. "The one you put him under."

"Yes, but which one is that?"

The manager stepped forward and kicked at the crate. "That one. I saw you."

"Would you like to pick the box up?" said Eddie.

The manager shrugged. "There'll be a dog underneath it."

He reached forward and lifted the box. There was nothing underneath it. "Well, I'll be darned," he said. "How did that dog get out of there?"

A bark came from underneath another crate. The manager walked over to it, lifted it up, and was greeted by the dog, who rushed forward to lick his hands.

"There's your dog," said Eddie.

The manager looked at him. "What else can you do?" he asked.

"I can saw a woman in half," said Eddie. "Not really, of course, but they'll think I have."

"I seen that once," said the manager. "Cut right through this dame and then she jumps up out of a suitcase. Amazing." He paused. "You'll need some stage clothes. I'll take you to Ruby. She'll fix you up."

Ruby was a woman in her mid-thirties. She had a friendly, open expression and Eddie liked her from the moment he met her.

"Ruby has a ventriloquism act," explained the manager. "She's the best ventriloquist in Western Canada."

"Oh, come on, George," said Ruby. "You don't want to be

confusing this young man. I do my best, but I'm certainly not the best."

"In my book you are," said the manager. "Anyway, Ruby, this young man is Eddie Beaulieu from Kingston, Ontario. He's just joined us. He's going to be doing a conjuring act and will need some clothes. Can you run something up for him?"

Ruby moved Eddie into the centre of the small workroom in which they had found her. She looked at him appraisingly. "Shouldn't be difficult," she said. "We've got a jacket that'll fit like a glove and I can take the trousers in a bit. Yes, I'll fix him up."

The manager left. Ruby reached for a bag and took out a tape measure. She measured his waist, wrote some figures down in a notebook, and then looked at her watch. "I usually have a cup of tea at about this time. Over in my trailer. You can come and meet Frank."

"Is he your husband?" asked Eddie.

"Gracious, no," said Ruby. "I just make tea for Frank and some of the boys, if they happen to be around. I think the others have gone off to get some animal feed. It'll just be Frank."

They walked round the side of the warehouse to where the trailers were parked. Ruby's was painted green and had a set of polished metal steps outside it. She ushered Eddie in.

Frank was sitting on a folding canvas chair. He was a man about the same age as Ruby, and had a large white hat balanced on one knee. Ruby introduced them.

"Frank," she said, "you tell Eddie what you do."

"I got a lion," said Frank. "I show him. And I got a dwarf—a musical dwarf. I'm his agent. He can't look after himself because he's not quite . . ." He tapped his head.

"He plays great music," said Ruby. "He has a tuba which is a bit bigger than he is. He plays it real well."

"They like that," said Frank. "They laugh fit to burst when Charles comes in. You should hear them."

Ruby lit the gas stove under the kettle. "Some people say that it's cruel, but it isn't, you know. Charles loves the attention."

"And he makes good money," said Frank. "I take ten per cent—not a dollar more. And I look after him."

Ruby was at pains to confirm this. "Charles couldn't do without Frank, Eddie. He gets into trouble with the cops, you see."

"We don't talk about that, Ruby." He turned to Eddie. "It

doesn't happen very often, but sometimes Charles gets a bit excited and we have to square it with the cops. He doesn't really mean any harm."

"If it wasn't for Frank," said Ruby, "Charles could easily be in prison." She paused. "Somebody said they've got a jail for dwarves up in the Yukon somewhere. You heard that, Frank?"

"Could be," said Frank.

"Small cells," said Ruby.

Tea was poured. Eddie told them about the act he was hoping to do. He went on to say a little bit about Pelmanism.

"Sounds interesting," said Ruby, glancing at Frank.

"I reckon so," said Frank.

Then Ruby said, "You'd better meet Harold."

"Yes," said Frank. "Harold is a very important fellow. He'll be dying to meet you."

Ruby went to a large cupboard and opened the door.

"Here's Harold," she said.

Harold was a ventriloquist's doll of classic appearance—rosy-cheeked, wide-eyed, and wearing a smart morning suit. She sat down with Harold on her knee, her arm up the back of Harold's jacket.

"So who is this young man?" asked Harold, in a high-pitched voice.

"This here is Eddie," said Ruby.

Harold's eyes widened. Mechanically operated eyelashes fluttered. "Very pleased to meet you, young fellow," he said. "You ever been kissed?"

"Harold!" scolded Ruby.

"I was only asking," said Harold, his mechanical lips moving in time to his words. "A smart young fellow like him, all the girls going to want to kiss him!"

"Yes, but you don't have to spell it out," said Frank.

"You shut your trap!" snapped Harold.

"Cupboard for you," said Ruby, rising to her feet. She bundled Harold into the cupboard and closed the door.

"That's a great act," Eddie complimented her. "I didn't see your lips moving at all."

"That's why she's the best," said Frank. "Everywhere we go, they love her. Edmonton, Calgary, down in Washington State. There isn't a place that doesn't love Ruby."

"You're too kind to me," said Ruby. "Why don't you go and introduce Eddie to Mackenzie King?"

"My lion," said Frank. "Would you like to meet him, Eddie?"

He saw the look of puzzlement on Eddie's face. "Yes, same name as the Prime Minister. William Lyon Mackenzie

King, except he—my lion—spells it William *Lion* Mackenzie King—Lion with an *i*."

Ruby broke out laughing. "Frank doesn't give the audience the full name, you see—some of them might think it disrespectful. So he just introduces him as *King*, and nobody bats an eyelid."

Eddie smiled. "Great joke," he said.

"Well, I think so," said Frank.

"He wouldn't hurt a fly," said Frank. "Look at him. Lazy piece of work."

Eddie approached the bars of the cage somewhat gingerly. The lion was lying on the floor of his cage, his eyes closed, his tail flicking at flies.

"I brought him up from San Diego," said Frank. "He'd lived there for four years. He was born in Texas, they said. Down in El Paso. They live up to twenty years in captivity, these creatures. Out in the wild they only get ten, twelve years maybe. Depends on their luck."

Eddie watched the lion. One of his eyes was opening now. It was a strange, tawny colour, thought Eddie: just the colour you would expect a lion's eye to be.

"I get him to jump on to a stool," said Frank. "Then he

leaps through a hoop. That's about it, I suppose." He paused. "I never use fire. Some guys use fire—but that terrifies them, you know. A lion hates fire more than anything else. It's cruel to make them jump through burning rings. I've got no time for that."

Eddie agreed. "That's a great name you've given him. It suits him."

Frank smiled. "I never liked that fellow Mackenzie King," he said. "Something about him. Don't know what it is."

Eddie was silent.

"And you?" asked Frank. "You like him back east?"

Eddie hesitated. "I could tell you something," he said.

"Oh yes? What?"

Eddie lowered his voice although they were alone. "He's in touch with the other side."

Frank frowned. "With the Opposition? The Conservative Party? I guess the Liberals have to talk to them . . ."

Eddie shook his head. "No, not the other political side . . . *the* other side. You know? When you die you go over to the other side. *That* other side."

"Oh, I see. You mean he's a . . . what do you call them folks? A spiritualist?"

"Yes," said Eddie. "I'm not criticising him for it, of course. I don't think you should close your mind to things like that."

Frank was suspicious. "How do you know? I never saw anything about that in the papers—at least not over here."

"There hasn't been anything," said Eddie. "I know because I've met the lady who tells his fortune."

Frank still looked doubtful. "Lots of people make things up, you know."

"Not her," said Eddie. "I know her because she lives in Kingston. I met her at a fair—she was telling fortunes. She's called Mrs. Bleaney. I asked her to teach me, and she did. I went to her place a lot and I learned all about fortune-telling. She called me her young disciple."

"And Mackenzie King goes there? To her place?"

Eddie nodded. "She says that he comes in private. She tells him what to do."

Frank gasped. "Hold on—you're telling me that this fortune-teller in Kingston tells the Prime Minister of Canada what to do?"

"Yes," said Eddie. He sounded defensive. "Except sometimes it doesn't work out very well. Fortune-tellers can make mistakes—same as anyone else."

"And she did?"

"Yes, she said to me that she had told Mackenzie King he'd win an election, and he didn't."

Frank clapped his hands together with delight. "They don't like that, those guys in Ottawa. They don't like that, do they?"

"She probably just misheard," said Eddie. "Sometimes the people on the other side can be indistinct."

Frank's eyes narrowed. "Really? You think that?"

"Oh, there's a lot of proof of that," said Eddie.

5

They toured British Columbia for six weeks. Eddie's act proved popular, eliciting gasps of astonishment from the audience as he made the human cannonball's dog disappear and then reappear in a totally unexpected place. Occasionally he would do the same with a child, if there were a suitable volunteer from the audience, but the manager eventually vetoed that after a mother became distraught, believing her child really had dematerialised.

After a month, Mr. Vink, who had returned to Toronto,

wrote to Mr. Beaulieu and said that he would not be required to send any further money. "The report I have from my manager over there is that your boy is doing really well," he said. "I shall take over the payment of his salary now and I shall wire back the sum you have just sent me. He is worth every cent, they tell me." This was followed by some news of his stomach. "I'm feeling so much better, you'll be pleased to hear. I can eat anything I fancy (not that I do, mind) and that acidic feeling I had is a thing of the past."

Mr. Beaulieu showed the letter to his wife. He found it difficult to believe, but it seemed that Eddie had found what he was looking for.

"He's obviously working hard," Mrs. Beaulieu said. "But do you think he's happy, Aristide?"

Mr. Beaulieu shrugged. "What's happiness?" he asked. "You ever found a good definition of it?"

Had they asked Eddie that question, they would have had an uncomplicated answer. Happiness, he thought, was being able to do what you want to do—and what he was now doing was exactly what he had always wished to do. After each performance, with the audience's applause ringing in his ears, he felt almost as if he had to pinch himself. This is *me*, he thought; they're clapping *me*.

The friends he had made right at the beginning, when he had first joined the circus in New Westminster, continued to be good friends. Frank only very occasionally asked for his help—mostly with collecting meat from the butcher for William Lion Mackenzie King—or occasionally with some small maintenance chore. As his conjuring act became more and more popular, the manager relieved him of his ticket collecting and clearing-up duties and assigned these, instead, to a boy whom they had engaged in Calgary—a sullen youth with an angry, pock-marked skin and shifty eyes.

Eddie told this youth's fortune for him. "You're going to get into trouble," he said, pointing to a line on the boy's hand. "Big trouble, it seems."

"What's new?" muttered the boy.

He struck up a friendship with the dwarf, who also asked for his fortune to be told. "You're going to be big," said Eddie, hastily correcting himself. "I mean, your career will be big."

The dwarf looked at him reproachfully.

"And rich," said Eddie quickly. "Look at this fortune line. See that? That tells us everything we need to know. There's big money coming your way."

Charles told Eddie something about himself. "I've been entertaining since I was ten," he said. "My father left home and I had to earn money to keep my mother. She's too small to work. Mind you, I'm not complaining. I have a good time. I get to laugh a lot and I make good money." He paused, and pushed his hand back towards Eddie. "Do you see anything there about the police?" he asked.

Eddie looked. "No, nothing."

"You darn sure?"

"Yes, I'm darn sure. There's nothing there about the police. Nothing."

"Good," said Charles. "That's the way I like it." Then he said, "Ruby? What do you think of her, Eddie?"

"I like her."

Charles nodded. "You think she likes you?"

"I hope so," said Eddie.

"Well," said the dwarf, "I can tell you something. Ruby thinks you're great. She said as much to me. She said, 'Eddie's great.' Those were her exact words."

Eddie beamed with pleasure. So Ruby thought highly of him? Well, the feeling was entirely reciprocated. He admired Ruby. He liked her cheerful expression; he liked her sense of humour. He liked the way she made up witty remarks for Harold, no matter what the context was. He admired her style.

Was it possible, he wondered, that Ruby liked him in *that way*? He found the idea intriguing—and exciting. She was quite a bit older than him, of course, but he did not think that mattered. Older women were far more interesting than those vacuous girls of eighteen or nineteen. They were just interested in their appearance, he felt. They thought about their clothes and their complexion all the time; they never read anything about anything. They were a lost cause to Pelmanism—they wouldn't have the sticking power. Useless girls. Useless.

Ruby and Frank discussed Eddie's progress.

"You know something, Rube?" Frank remarked one evening. "Young Eddie's born for this particular life. He's got *circus* written all over him. What do you think?"

They were sitting in Ruby's trailer, passing the hour or so before the show was due to begin in the drinking of tea and catching up on the day's events. Ruby made sandwiches for these occasions, including the egg and cress sandwiches that were Frank's one major weakness.

"You're right, Frank," she said. "Some people have it—others don't."

"You could probably say that about most jobs, of course,"

said Frank. "Those folks over in Ottawa, for instance. They need to be a certain type of person. Mackenzie King, for instance—not our Mackenzie King, of course—the Prime Minister. He must want to be Prime Minister. He must love it."

"He works hard enough to keep it," said Ruby.

"Poor fellow," mused Frank. "He's lost so many members of his family. He must be mighty lonely up there. Driven him to this spiritualism stuff, Eddie says."

"Eddie? What does he know about it?"

"Apparently he knows this woman in Kingston who's a medium of some sort. She says the Prime Minister comes to see her regularly. Gets his fortune told. Eddie's interested in that stuff."

Ruby shook her head. "Leave well alone, I always say."

"I'm inclined to agree," said Frank.

"He needs to meet somebody, Frank. He needs to meet a girl. I've seen it so often, you know—a young man takes himself too seriously, goes on about something, and then he meets a girl and you don't hear much more from him."

Frank wondered whether Pelmanism would be forgotten if Eddie met a girl. Was that what Ruby meant?

"Yes," she said. "Girls aren't interested in Pelmanism,

Frank. He'd learn pretty quickly not to talk about it if he met a nice girl."

Ruby lapsed into silence, prompting an enquiry from Frank: "You all right, Rube?"

"Thinking," she said, and then, "Jack's got a niece, you know. Over in Saskatoon. She's about Eddie's age—maybe a bit younger. Jack tells me that her parents are keen to find a suitable young man for her. They haven't had much luck up to now."

Jack was the human cannonball.

"Do you think you could try to get them together?" Frank asked.

"I don't see why not," said Ruby. "I'll have a word with Jack. He likes Eddie, you know."

"I believe Eddie told him he had a great future," Frank said. "Not that I'm suggesting that's the reason why Jack likes him. But it helps, I think. Somebody comes along and tells you you've got a great future . . . well, it's human nature, isn't it?"

Ruby laughed. "The other day he asked if he could tell my fortune."

"And?"

She shrugged. "Well, I agreed. I don't believe any of that. Gypsies and so on. Tarot cards."

"But you said he could?"

"Why not? He's going to do it tomorrow, he told me. Innocent fun, Frank." She reached for the plate of sandwiches. "Another sandwich?"

"You spoil me."

"And why not?"

Frank looked about him. He loved the comfort of Ruby's trailer. He liked the neat antimacassars on the chairs. He liked the way that she made the trailer into a home. It was just a basic trailer, a cart really, but she transformed it into something much more than that. Somebody—one of the dancers, he thought—had said to him that there was a German word to describe the atmosphere that Ruby's trailer created. *Gemütlichkeit*. It was a great word—if you could get your mouth about it.

"All right," said Ruby. "I'm ready."

Eddie sat himself in front of her. His chair was slightly lower than hers, and that meant he was looking up into her face. In ordinary circumstances he would not have liked that—being lower than the person whose fortune he was telling—but it did not seem to matter with Ruby.

"Can you give me your hand, please?"

Ruby stretched out her right hand, and Eddie took it. His touch was slightly damp, she thought, but then the weather was hot and everybody was damp. She watched as he examined her palm, bending his head forward to peer at the lines and creases. *I must get a gentler soap,* she thought. *You have to watch what soap does to your skin—it could change your whole future!*

"You're smiling," said Eddie. "What's the joke?"

"Just something I thought of," said Ruby. "Sorry, I didn't mean to put you off your stride."

"That's all right," said Eddie. "Pelmanism teaches you to concentrate. That's one of its big things, you know."

"I must read about it some day," said Ruby.

"I've got a pamphlet," said Eddie. "I can bring it round . . ."

She cut him off. "Not just yet, Eddie. I'm reading Dickens. It's a big book. Some other time, perhaps." She paused. "Now this hand of mine—what do you see? Am I going to be rich?"

Eddie shook his hand. "Not rich, no. Nor poor, really. You see this line here? That's wealth. Yours goes down there, but it's not as long as some I've seen. I'd say that you're going to be comfortably off. Yes, that's probably the best way of putting it."

"Well, who would have known?" said Ruby.

"Your life line's good," said Eddie. "It's this one here. You're going to have a good, long life."

Ruby chuckled. "That's a relief. I wouldn't want to think I'd be run over by a train next week."

"The hand doesn't give such specific information," said Eddie. There was a note of reproach in his voice.

"Sorry," said Ruby. "It's just that I felt quite relieved to hear what you had to say about that."

"That's understandable," said Eddie.

He turned her wrist slightly and the pressure of his fingers increased. She felt an urge to withdraw her hand, but did not do so. One of his fingers was moving slightly, as if stroking her. She frowned, and the movement stopped.

"This line is all about love," said Eddie, pointing with his free hand. "You will meet somebody who really loves you and you'll ask him to marry you—no, I meant: he'll ask you to marry him. And you must marry him. When the question comes, you must say yes, because he loves you very dearly and he'll make a good husband for you."

She caught her breath. "Tell me about him," she said—and then immediately regretted it. *I should end this now.*

"He's a bit younger than you," said Eddie. "You may already have met him, I think . . . Let me look closer . . . Yes, I think you have."

She withdrew her hand. He tried to keep hold of it, but his own hand had become sweatier, and it slipped. She rose to her feet, adjusting her skirt.

"Well, Eddie," she said cheerfully. "That was a very interesting experience. I'm glad that my future is not entirely bleak."

He seemed flustered.

"I've made some sandwiches," she said. "And a pot of tea. I'll give Frank a shout—I'm sure he'll want to join us."

Eddie fingered his collar. "I didn't really finish the reading," he said.

She was firm. "Some other time . . . maybe."

When Frank arrived the atmosphere of slight tension seemed to dissipate. William Lion Mackenzie King was off his food for some reason, and that became the topic of conversation.

"Give him a dose of salts," suggested Eddie.

Frank asked whether animals responded to a dose of salts in the same way as humans. "Can you give salts to animals?"

"Yes," said Eddie. "My uncle's dog was always getting these turns, you see. I told my uncle to give him salts. He did, and he always got better."

"I could try," said Frank. "But with him off his food, how am I going to get the salts into him?"

"In his water," said Eddie.

"I've made sandwiches," said Ruby.

Frank brightened. "Egg and cress?"

"Specially for you," said Ruby, smiling at him.

Eddie watched. She didn't listen, he thought. She didn't listen. That was the problem with so many people—they didn't listen. That's why they needed Pelmanism to help them. If more people did Pelmanism, then more of them would listen. It was so obvious.

6

On their second night in Calgary, immediately after a show to a packed tent, fire broke out among the wagons and trailers. The cause was uncertain, and the damage was relatively light—it could have been far worse had the fire started while people were still in the tent. As it was, the fire trucks reached them within minutes and extinguished the blaze before it could take hold. A large truck used for storing seating was destroyed and so was Ruby's trailer. She was not in it at the time, as she had a cousin in Calgary and she had gone off to spend the night in her house.

They had no means of contacting her. When she returned the following morning, she saw Frank standing outside the charred shell of her trailer, along with the manager and the human cannonball. She screamed, and Frank spun round. He ran to meet her.

"We don't know what happened," he said. "Probably a cigarette tossed down by some passer-by—smoulders away and then, well . . . thank heavens you weren't in it."

She entered the charred ruins of the trailer—a barely recognisable mass of twisted metal, ash, and fragments of glass.

"Harold," she muttered.

Frank took her hand. "I found him," he said.

He led her away. On a small table erected by the manager, the burned frame of the ventriloquist's doll was laid out, like a human victim of a conflagration. The wires that had been used to operate his limbs and his lips were twisted into a blackened bundle.

"I'm so sorry about this," said the manager. "It must be a real loss to you."

She said nothing. She reached out to touch what had been Harold's head. Her fingers came away blackened. She rubbed these against her skirt, marking it.

"What do you want to do?" whispered Frank.

She shrugged. "Carry on, I suppose."

"That's the spirit," said the manager. "We all carry on."

She shot him a glance, and he looked away quickly.

The human cannonball came up to her and put an arm round her shoulder. "He was a great prop, Harold was," he said. "He wouldn't have known anything about it. The heat was very intense."

Her mouth twisted. "Thank you, Jack," she said.

The manager had an idea. "There'll be an insurance claim," he said. "It will more than cover a new doll."

She nodded her thanks. "I just want to cry," she said quietly. "I just want to cry by myself." But then she looked up sharply. "What about tonight? What about the show?"

Frank stroked his chin. "Come along with me, Rube. I've got a suggestion."

He looked at the manager, who nodded his assent.

They walked off, watched by Eddie. He had wanted to say something, but had been unable to find the words.

That night was the first time that Frank and Ruby did their act together. They had had no idea that it would be so successful, but the near-hysterical laughter of the audience and the thunderous applause at the end of their act left no doubt in anybody's mind: they had stumbled upon a whole new approach to ventriloquism.

The concept was simple. Frank played the part of the ventriloquist's doll, and perched on Ruby's lap in exactly the same way as Harold had done. She then engaged in conversation with him in which he merely opened and shut his mouth, leaving the speaking to her. What produced the laughter, though, was the occasional spontaneous movement from Frank—wave to the audience, a wink, a pulling of the tongue—while Ruby was looking elsewhere. This just happened to work.

At the end of the first performance the manager came to congratulate them in Ruby's temporary trailer.

"We have just witnessed," he said, "the inauguration of the greatest ventriloquist act in Canadian history."

"I'm glad you liked it," said Frank. "It was just a piece of nonsense, really."

"Liked it?" the manager exploded. "I *loved* it!"

Harold was never replaced—there was no need. Frank, described in the circus programme as Oscar, the Almost Human, continued in his supporting role, perched on Ruby's lap, a perfect foil for her wit. He still continued to show William Lion Mackenzie King, but that act never provided him with anything like the enjoyment he derived from his role as Oscar. "It's the difference between vaudeville and Shakespeare," he said to friends. "One pays the rent, the other is art."

A month after the fire, when they were on tour over the border in Washington State, Frank asked Eddie to come to his trailer.

"I want to talk to you in private," he said.

Eddie was uneasy; he had a good idea what Frank wanted to talk to him about, and he was correct.

"I think you should know that Rube and I are getting hitched," said Frank.

Eddie bit his lip. "I see . . ."

"And I want you to be best man," said Frank. "I hope you can accept."

Eddie closed his eyes. This was the biggest challenge his Pelmanism had ever faced. He had to remain calm.

"That's mighty kind of you, Frank. Of course I'd be delighted to do that for you."

Frank looked relieved. "We're not going to leave it long. Two weeks from now we'll be in Spokane. We'll get a judge up there to marry us."

Eddie swallowed hard. "That'll be good." It cost him a great effort to say that, but he did it again when he said, "I'm really pleased."

Frank went with him to congratulate Ruby. She gave Eddie a hug, and felt him withdrawn and stiff with sorrow.

"You were right, Eddie," she gushed. "You said I'd already met the man I would marry—and I had! You said he would be a bit younger than me, and Frank is exactly two months younger! It's all there in the palm isn't it? You were absolutely right!"

And so, two weeks later, they appeared before a judge in Spokane. It was a hot afternoon, and the wind on those high plains was dry and persistent.

"Where do you think the wind comes from?" said Ruby. "You know the answer to that, Eddie?"

He turned his head. The warm wind was on his face. If he had tears to shed—and he did—then they would be quickly dried by that wind.

"The wind comes from a happier place," whispered Ruby. "That's where it comes from."

He took the photograph. Frank sat on her lap, wearing his best white Stetson. "You happy, Oscar?" she asked. And from Frank's closed mouth came the reply, "Very happy, love."

7

On the last day of July in 1998, the *Kingston Whig-Standard* carried this short obituary:

> The death at 98 last Saturday of Edward Beaulieu robs the Canadian circus world of one of its most distinguished sons. Edward Beaulieu was the son of a fur trapper turned tax accountant, Aristide Beaulieu, and his wife, Hope Beaulieu (née Patterson). As a young man

he joined the Great All-Canada Circus in BC and soon established a reputation for mounting one of the best sleight of hand acts in North America.

Beaulieu married Miss Gwen Torrent of Saskatoon, a niece of another well-known circus performer, Jack Torrent, known as the human cannonball. It was a long and happy marriage and the couple saw their Golden Anniversary together.

Beaulieu was a generous man, given to telling fortunes. He tried to tailor fortunes to the needs of those who consulted him, and few were sent away disappointed. His life was not without incident, including one occasion when he unwisely attempted to read the lines on the paw of a circus lion named King. The injuries he sustained as a result of this required a three-week enforced recuperation period at Lake Louise, during which Beaulieu began the writing of his one and only book, *The Future Lies in the Past*, eventually published in Toronto by Douglas Gibson five years ago.

His wife having predeceased him, and there being no children, Beaulieu left his entire estate to the Pelmanism Institute of Southern Ontario.

He was a good man.

The Woman with the Beautiful Car

I

On a chilly spring morning in 1913 in the west of Ireland, a young man assisted in the changing of a car's wheel. The car was being driven by Roger Kelly, by night a consummate poacher, by day employed by the father of the young woman in the white double-breasted coat. Her name was Anthea, and she was the daughter of a successful speculative builder, Thomas Farrell, who, having made a fortune in Dublin, had retired to an estate in the country. Thomas was aware that Roger took most of the fish from his trout stream, but turned a blind eye to this, as Roger had proved himself indispensable in so many ways. These included being the only man able to humour their car out of its habit of stalling at awkward moments.

The car was a 1907 Standard Tourer, made in a factory in Coventry, and briefly owned by an exiled Irishman in Manchester who used it for a trip to Galway. Unfortunately, he had died on the journey—"expired while travelling," as his newspaper obituary put it. The car was stolen by the proprietor of the hotel in which its owner had died, and subsequently repainted and sold to Thomas Farrell. He had no idea that he was purchasing a stolen vehicle, and would have been appalled at the thought: he had always prided himself on the honesty—and general integrity—of his business dealings in Dublin. "They may say that I built slums," he said. "But I built *decent* slums, so I did!"

Thomas was proud of his Standard Tourer. "It's a real beauty of a car," he said to his daughter. "Look at the seats, darling. Buttoned leather, with velvet trimmings. Just like one of those grand sofas, those . . . those . . ."

"Chesterfields."

"Yes, Chesterfields. Look at them. And you see the high window at the front? See it? That's called the windscreen, and the wood it's made of is ash. The very best ash from some forest over in England. They make fine cars, the English—fine cars."

She had not been particularly interested in these details, but enjoyed riding in the car, perched on the high passenger seat with the hood down and the sun on her face, although more frequently it was rain—that thin, drifting rain that fell in veils over their slice of Irish countryside.

Thomas Farrell had little use for the car, as he rarely went anywhere. There were occasions, though, when he was invited to other country houses, and since he was trying to establish himself with the gentry of the area, it was important that he should arrive in style. His acceptance in the county, though, would always be half-hearted, as he failed every test that such circles applied, from religion to his table manners. In his undoubted favour, though, was the fact that he owned two thousand acres, and some of those acres were good shooting country, with pheasants and woodcock in abundance.

"A touch of the *gombeen*," said one neighbour to another. "But such are the times we live in."

"Not a bad fellow," replied the other. "Close your eyes and block your ears and he passes with flying colours."

Thomas was a widower, and Anthea was his only close family, apart from his two brothers in Cork, from whom he was largely estranged. He had waved olive branch after olive branch in their direction, to very little avail. One had borrowed money from him and never paid it back; the other had some vague, ancient complaint against him, dating back even into their childhood—something to do with a bicycle—the details of which now evaded even the bearer of the grudge.

Anthea had been educated at a small school for girls in Dublin. She had then been sent to England for a year, to a finishing school in Cheltenham, where young women were given instruction in deportment, French, and a few other subjects thought to be helpful in making a good marriage. As if to confirm this, she had received a proposal from the brother of one of her friends at this school, but had been put off him by the friend herself.

"William is quite useless," the friend had warned. "I should know, as I've known him all my life. He would not make a good husband. In fact, the only place for him is the army."

"Oh . . ."

"Indian Army," continued the friend. "And here's another thing: my father feels exactly the same way. William is a great disappointment to him."

It was unambiguous advice, and Anthea followed it.

"You're so kind," she said to William. "But I must go back to Ireland, as my father needs me there. I'm sure you will find a nice girl soon, and you will be very happy."

"I would have been very happy with you, you know. More than happy."

"That's as may be, but I have made up my mind. I'm so sorry."

He went into the army, as Anthea's friend had predicted, although he did not go to India. In August, 1914, two days after he reached France as a young lieutenant, and within the first hour of his arrival at the front, he was shot dead at the battle of Le Cateau.

2

The young man helping to change the wheel was called Ronald O'Carroll. He was twenty-five at the time, and he was the teacher in the small National School in the nearby village. This school had only eighteen pupils, and Ronald ran it single-handed, although the Board of Education occasionally gave him a temporary assistant to help with the younger children. He had succeeded his father in the post: George O'Carroll had taught there for thirty years before he and his wife retired to a house left to him by an uncle in Sligo. Ronald, who had just finished at university, stepped right into his father's shoes, not only taking up the job he had vacated, but moving back to the teacher's house in which he had spent his childhood. This house adjoined the school, its vegetable plot being separated from the children's playground by no more than a flimsy fence.

"Some men don't go very far," said a woman in the village. "Will you look at that Ronald O'Carroll: raised in that school, sent off to Dublin for an education, so he was, and then right back where he started."

"True," said her friend. "But then he's a nice young fellow—very good-looking, he is—and he'll meet somebody soon enough. That'll get him out of that school. I don't think we need to worry too much about Ronald O'Carroll."

3

There had been an overlap of two weeks between his return from Dublin and his parents' departure for Sligo. It had been a strange spell for him, as they were living in the same house, with him occupying the same room that he had occupied as a boy, with his mother still cooking his meals exactly as she had done for as long as he could remember, and his father sitting in the same chair, smoking the same pipe that he had always smoked—one bowl a day, after dinner, filling the room with acrid tobacco fumes. It seemed to him that the same things were said too—things he had heard ever since he had begun to take notice of such matters—comments on the latest instructions from the

Board and on the iniquities of the British government. His father made no secret of his sympathies, although as the teacher he was expected to be discreet. "There'll never be peace until we see the back of them," he said. "Home Rule will just be the start. Then we can show them the door."

Ronald shrugged. "And Ulster?"

"Hot air," said his father. "Huffing and puffing. Carson and those fellows need to be taken by the scruff of the neck. If London thinks it's the boss, then bring it home to them. But do they do that? No, because too many of them are in cahoots with them. They put them up to it. They egg them on, you know. They're all over the shop."

Ronald did not engage. Political discussion did not interest him. He liked poetry.

"This man, Yeats," George said to Ronald when he returned from Dublin. "Did you ever see him in Dublin?"

"Twice. Once in a hall. He read some of his works and I bought a ticket. Then I saw him in the street near St. Stephen's Green."

"Well, would you believe that? Walking along like any ordinary fellow?"

"Yes."

His father stared out of the window. "He has the right idea, so he does. Him and that brother of his—the one who paints. They have the right idea."

It was an expression he used frequently—a general term of approbation—applied to those whose views accorded with his. Such people had the right idea, whereas those with whom he disagreed were "all over the shop."

Ronald looked at his father. In a few days he would be away to Sligo and Ronald would be here in this house by himself, the teacher, and his life would stretch out before him; a life of educating the children of the people his father had taught, sighing over the same families with whom little progress could be made—those Severins, for instance, with their thick necks and their dirty fingernails and their bovine acceptance of their lot. What was the point of teaching them? They went back to their unwashed ways the moment they left the school, never looking at the printed word, never thinking about anything except their fields and their ill-tempered pigs, and the wives they recruited down in West Cork and brought back to perpetuate the dynasty.

He saw that his father was looking at him, and he felt a flush of embarrassment. They had never talked very much about things that mattered—about what he wanted out of life, and how he felt about that place and the people he lived with, and about roads not taken.

"One of these days," his father said hesitantly, "you might even get yourself married. I'm not saying tomorrow, of course—just one of these days."

"Oh, Da . . ."

"No, don't just say *Oh, Da,* because you'll need to, you know. You can't live here by yourself for ever. Who's going to cook for you? Who's going to launder your shirts?"

"I can cook for myself. I know how to fry an egg. And as for my shirts . . . what's wrong with washing your own shirts?"

This brought a shaking of the head. "Mrs. Mason won't like that. You'll be doing her out of a job."

"I didn't say anything about that. She can stay. I've told her that. I'll pay her exactly what you and Ma paid her."

"For less work? There'll only be one of you."

"It doesn't matter."

His father was thinking. "That girl, the postmaster's daughter—the one who went to Galway for a few years and then came back. She's a nice girl."

"I dare say she is."

"Dark hair and that skin . . . how would you describe it? Translucent."

"If it was translucent you'd see her veins. You'd see the blood vessels underneath. It wouldn't be very pleasant. You'd have to say, *What lovely blood vessels you've got.*"

His father smiled, in spite of himself. "You may laugh," he said. "But I'm telling you, Ronald: I've seen many a man living by himself go mad. It's what happens. Slowly, sure enough—but it happens."

"Name one. Go on—name one."

His father closed his eyes. "You may think you know better than me. I didn't go to Dublin, but I know a thing or two."

"Of course you do, Da. I'd never say you didn't."

"Then listen to me. That's all I ask: listen to my advice."

He lay awake at night and thought of his life. At university he had mixed with people with a strong sense of where they were going, who were in no doubt about what they wanted to achieve and had already identified the milestones on that journey. He stood in awe of them—of the would-be bankers and lawyers, the aspiring civil servants, the company men who knew that in ten years' time or even earlier they would be earning enough to own their own houses, belong to golf clubs, and support wives and children. By contrast, he would be living in a house that went with the job, not much better off than he was now. He would be able to afford to marry, but there would be precious little money left over once the household bills were paid. That was how his parents had lived, and it seemed that was how he would too.

A couple of days before his parents were due to depart for Sligo, he awoke at three in the morning. He had heard that time of day being called the *hour of the wolf*—a time of utter loneliness when every man is a stranger in the world, unhappy with the present and dreading the future. He lay in the darkness, shifting slightly to find the most comfortable contours in the mattress that had seen him through boyhood; when his parents left, he would move into the bed they had occupied for much of their married lives—the bed in which he had, in fact, been born. That thought, more than any other, depressed him.

He made his decision, and lit the candle by his bedside because he wanted to see whether the idea would survive light, even the flickering illumination of a single candle. It did. He would tell his parents tomorrow. He would offer to stay, of course, until the Board found a new teacher, so it would not delay his father's retirement, but once that was done he would pack up and return to Dublin. One of the friends he had made at university had said that his father had a business that was expanding and could offer him a job if he ever needed one. He would contact him—even send him a telegram to tell him that he was coming back.

"I don't want to stand in your way," said his father. "I've never done that, and I won't do that now."

"I know that, Da. Thank you."

His father looked at him, moving his glasses on the bridge of his nose; things were cloudier now than they used to be, and he would have to submit at some point to the operation that he so dreaded. "But I can't understand why you want to give everything up. You'll be all over the shop."

"It's not giving things up. It's making a change. There are all sorts of opportunities in Dublin."

It was as if he had not been heard. "Why do you want to go off to London? A fellow can't have much of a life there."

"I said nothing about London. I said Dublin."

His father looked away. "The trouble with living in those places is that there are too many people with the same idea. Out here, you have the sky above you, the place to yourself, and a decent meal waiting for you at night." He paused. "You can put a bit of money aside each month. You can be comfortable enough."

"I'd like a bit of a challenge. All you say may be true, but I'd still like a bit of a challenge."

This brought a wounded look. "So you think there's no challenge? You think it isn't a challenge to provide an education for these children? To make something of these . . . these little souls? To give them a chance—the only chance they're going to get in this life, as likely as not? That's not a challenge?"

He reached out to put a hand on his father's shoulder. "I appreciate what you've done, and I'm sure they do." He thought of the Severins. One of the boys had been sent off to Letterfrack Industrial School for reasons that had not been made clear; they would sort him out there, his father had said, but he doubted it because he had not seen anybody improved by the cruelty meted out in such places. Shortly he would have three Severins under his care, trying to keep them from falling asleep in the classroom or stealing from the other children. Would anybody appreciate that? Would anybody even know about it?

His father took out his pipe and filled it with a plug of tobacco. "Couldn't you give it a year? Just a year, so that people don't think that I've just walked away from this place?"

Ronald tried to reassure him. "Nobody will think that. How could they?"

"Oh, they will, you know. Father Morrissey for one. The people on the Board. Everybody, really."

He looked at his father's hands, tanned brown from the work that he did in the garden. He often looked at people's hands and wondered about the work they had done.

"Do you really want me to?"

His father hesitated. "Yes. Just a year. Then you can leave honourably. We will have done our duty by the school."

4

His mother wrote to him from Sligo. "My dear Ronald, your father and I are very happy. I have never seen him more contented, as I hope you will agree, if you are able to come and see us at the end of this term. I think he has forgotten all about the school—already—after only seven weeks away! Can you believe that? For forty years, or close enough, it was his life, day in day out, and then in the space of a few weeks it was as if he had never been a teacher. I am astonished, but I think it's good for him to have a whole new life.

"He has been brushing up on his Irish. There is a man near here who has had some Irish poems published and they talk together. Your da says that his words are coming back to him. He says that they have always been there, but they have been asleep for a long time.

"There is a woman in the village called Brenda Hallissey. She is a very good dressmaker and is teaching me some of her skills. I am making a waistcoat for your da out of some material I found in the attic. It is very thick tweed and I have to be careful not to get the needle in my fingers, but it will be a very fine garment I think. Brenda says that I have a talent for this sort of thing, but I am not sure whether she is just being polite. They are very well mannered in these parts.

"Your da is planting potatoes and some beans too. He says that we can live off the land here once we get the garden broken in. The uncle let it go to weeds and it is taking a lot of time to get it sorted out. Your da says that we have all the time in the world now that he has retired, but I say that you never know when the Good Lord will decide it's time to go, and so I have told him not to waste time in getting his potatoes and beans in the ground.

"And make sure that you don't waste time either. You know what I mean by that: do not wait for ever. The man who waits for the right girl may find that the right girl has herself not been waiting. That's a thought—just a thought, but, like at least some thoughts, it happens to be true.

"Your ever-loving mother."

5

He first saw her when she drove past him on the road into the village. Because it had to serve another village as well, the school had been built between the two, so that the children of neither would be unduly favoured or inconvenienced. This meant that Ronald had a half hour's walk to do his shopping every Saturday morning. He enjoyed the walk, though, unless the rain was heavy, in which case he would take his bicycle, protected by the tent-like waterproof cycling cape that his father had used and had now passed on to him.

That Saturday was a fine day and he had been obliged to remove his jacket for the heat. Halfway through the journey, he had stopped at a place where the road for a brief time followed the shore of a lough, and there, under the shade of a rowan tree, he had sat on a half-buried boulder and looked out over the water. He was there for half an hour—he had plenty of time to reach the village before the shops closed at one o'clock; there was no need to hurry.

There were things to look at. Vetches—plants that as children they had known as *poor man's peas*—grew along the ground here, their tendrils reaching out for some stalk, some salience that would allow them to grow upwards. It was death to eat these peas, they said, and a dead cow in a field would as often as not be pointed to as a victim; but he knew—because his father had demonstrated it to him—this particular variety was harmless: bitter, yes, but not poisonous as legend claimed. There were rushes too, and snipe would sometimes rise up out of these, or perch on some stone or tuft and launch into their characteristic song that sounded so much like a squeaky door being moved backwards and forwards on its hinges.

He heard the approach of a car—a rare event, as there were few motor vehicles in the area, and if one were spotted, then everybody would be curious as to who it was. He craned his neck to give him a better view of the road, which was a good twenty yards away. The noise grew louder until, appearing from behind a rise in the ground, the car swept past him. He saw the driver, a man in a flat cap, and on the elevated seat behind, as if riding some winged chariot, a woman in a high-buttoned white coat. Her bonnet was kept in place by a veil tied over it and then fastened below her chin, but this was of light muslin and did not obscure her face to any great extent. She turned, and looked at him; she had not expected, he thought, to see a man under a tree in that remote spot, and he was sure he saw surprise in her expression. On instinct, he raised his hand. She returned the wave and then, in a cloud of dust thrown up from the unpaved road, the car disappeared from view.

He lowered his hand, still raised in salute, and in a sudden moment of needless embarrassment he saw that the thumbnail had a line of black dirt under it. He had dug out potatoes that morning, and although he had scrubbed his hands with a pumice stone, he had missed the earth under that nail. She could not have seen it, of course, but now he prised it out with the tip of his penknife blade. He felt warm. He felt his heart beating more quickly, as if to remind him that something special had happened.

He stood up and resumed his walk. Who was this young woman and where was she going? She had smiled at him as she waved, but that meant nothing, he knew; she would have smiled at anyone who waved to her from under a rowan tree in the middle of nowhere—of course she would.

. . .

At the grocery store, Heaney's, he asked about the car. "There was some sort of beautiful car went past this morning. A lovely piece of machinery. You wouldn't know whose it was, would you, Mr. Heaney?"

"A car with a young lady riding in the back?"

He nodded, casually, trying to create the impression that the question was not important.

The grocer was measuring flour, and he dusted his hands on his apron. "Now that would be Mr. Farrell. Well-off fellow. He bought that place up at Kilconnell—you know the one—ten miles over that way, maybe a bit more. Dublin man. Made a lot of money building houses."

"You'd need money to buy a car like that," said Ronald.

The grocer agreed. "But give me a jaunting car any time." He paused. "Why would you be asking?"

"Just interested. As I said, it was a beautiful car."

"And the girl too," said the grocer. "That's his daughter, Anthea. She comes in here from time to time, but not on Saturdays. She goes off then with a cousin to see some aunt or other. Every Saturday. Nice girl, I'm told."

He bought his supplies, packed them in the knapsack he had brought with him, and began the journey home. *Every*

Saturday . . . If he were to wait on the road next Saturday, he would see her again. He would wave, and it would be as if they were friends—of a sort. He wanted to meet her. He wanted to tell her about the school. He wanted to sit there by the shore of the lough and watch the snipe. He wanted to lie back and look at the sky with her, at its cloudlessness, and tell her how the sky made him dizzy to look at when it was empty like that; and tell her other things that he had nobody else to talk to about: how he missed the company of his father, and of his friends in Dublin; how he felt that while they were enjoying all the *craic,* life was passing him by in this small place; how it somehow seemed that life was a sentence we had to serve in whatever way we could, hoping at least for remission at some point along the journey.

Once back at the house, he put his supplies in the food cupboard and went to the small living room at the front of the house. The afternoon sun warmed this room, and he could sit there and read the newspaper he had picked up in the village—published the day before—and look up the hurling results, which he followed closely. A friend from schooldays played an active role in the Gaelic Athletic Association and was keen for him to do so too.

He put down the newspaper and rose from his chair.

He went outside, and stood for a while in the shadow of the house, feeling the breeze on his face. There was a smell of peat smoke, drifting from one of the houses further down the road; it was a smell that he had missed in Dublin, where coal, rather than turf, was used; it was a smell that reminded him that this was where he belonged. He felt unsettled—he had convinced himself that he could never stay in this place, but now he was not so sure.

He wondered if he could wait until Saturday to see her, but knew, of course, that he had no alternative but to do so. And it was while he was wrestling with this that he realised how he would be able to ensure that he met her next week. It was an outrageous notion, and he flushed with shame at the thought that he—the teacher—could do such a thing. It was almost as if the decision to act was being made by somebody else altogether—by some agency, some other presence, that was within him, operating through his mind, but at the same time nothing to do with him. This, he thought, is how it must feel to be possessed; to be aware that what you did was the act of something, some other person, within you that was not your real self, not the self that looked out on the world through your eyes when you awoke each morning, that accompanied you through the day, that experienced and remembered the things that happened to you, that whispered to you of memories, of love, of regret—of all that made us who we were.

He went that afternoon to the house of the local carpenter and his wife. They had two children in the school, and these children watched him through a chink in a door, awed by the presence of the teacher in their home on a Saturday afternoon.

"You fix furniture, don't you, Noel?"

The carpenter replied that he did.

"Upholstery too, I hear?"

Again the carpenter nodded. "You'll need to provide the fabric yourself."

"It's not that," he said. "I was wondering whether you could let me have some tacks. You use those, don't you?"

The carpenter left the room. Through the crack in the door the children watched him. He saw their shadows at the bottom of the door, thrown by the afternoon sun shining directly through the windows behind them.

"I know you're there, Padraig and Brigid," he said in a loud voice.

The shadows froze, and then the carpenter returned with a small paper bag. "There's about thirty in there," he said, handing the bag to him. "Will that be enough for whatever it is you're doing?" He paused. "I could come over and give you a hand, you know. There'd be no charge."

Ronald shook his head. "That's good of you," he said. "But not this time, I think."

6

It was cold for spring, and he hugged his knees as he sat and waited for the sound of the car. Mr. Heaney had said that she went every Saturday to visit her aunt, but he had not said anything about her going at the same time each week. Ronald was a creature of habit, who liked to keep to a routine, but not everybody was like that. She might have decided to go in the afternoon instead, or possibly in the evening, and he could hardly sit out there all day in that weather. He looked at his hands, and thought: *These are the hands of a criminal.* But then he put the thought out of his mind. *I'm not stealing anything or harming anybody, I'm simply . . .*

His thoughts were interrupted by the sound of an engine somewhere in the distance. It was a strained sound, as if it were struggling up a hill, but then it relaxed as the driver changed gear. Now it was louder. *Sit still,* he told himself. *Look the other way—gaze out at the water of the lough.*

He focused on a duck, an eider, that was leading a brood of early hatchlings in a sedate line across the surface of the water. He counted the ducklings. Six. And how many would survive the next few weeks? Two? One? In an attempt to keep his mind off the approaching car, he tried to envisage their fate: the fox, for whom they would be a tasty appetiser, a voracious rat, a harrier or other bird of prey.

He was thinking of birds of prey when he heard the popping sound. It was not very loud, but it was audible enough, and now he could legitimately stand up and look towards the road. The car had stopped, and the driver was climbing down from his elevated seat.

Ronald walked towards the road.

"Having a problem?" he called out. "Broken down?"

Roger Kelly turned round, surprised by his sudden appearance. "Blow-out," he said. "A flat tyre."

Ronald shook his head. "Can I help you change the wheel?"

Roger gestured towards the rear of the car. "Thank you. I'll get the jack and the spare."

Ronald saw that the young woman was getting out.

Another young woman—the cousin, he assumed—was with her.

"What is it, Mr. Kelly?"

"A flat tyre, miss. Easily fixed. Especially with some help." He nodded in the direction of Ronald, who smiled, and glanced at her shyly.

"That's very kind of you," said the young woman.

"Not at all," said Ronald as he stepped forward and offered his hand. She shook it.

"My name's Anthea Farrell," she said.

He gave her his name.

"You're the teacher at that school," she said. "The national school. That's you, isn't it?"

She looked down at the ground.

"I am," he said.

There was something in her expression that puzzled him. She seemed amused.

"You'd better help Mr. Kelly. I have my camera. I shall take a photograph of the lough."

"It's a fine view," he said.

She looked out over the water, as if seeing it for the first time. "I should like to walk round it one day. Have you done that?"

He felt the back of his neck becoming warm. "I have," he said. "I could show you, if you like."

"I would like that."

"Tomorrow?" he said.

She adjusted her veil. "I think that would be very pleasant. We could fetch you in the car." She looked at the driver, who threw a glance in Ronald's direction. "Well, Mr. Kelly?"

He nodded. "As you say, miss."

She smiled at Ronald. "Eleven o'clock in the morning?"

"That would be perfect."

"Unless, of course, you'll be at Mass then."

"I shall go earlier," he said quickly.

He helped Roger Kelly replace the wheel with the spare. While they worked, both Anthea and her cousin took photographs. As the punctured wheel was laid aside, the driver ran his hand over the tyre. "Two tacks," he said curtly. "You see? Here and here. Unusual, that."

Ronald peered at the tacks as they were extracted from the tyre. "You'd think people would be more careful," he muttered.

The driver looked at him sideways.

7

Three months later, when summer was beginning to tilt towards autumn, the Standard Tourer, driven by Roger Kelly and with Thomas Farrell sitting on the buttoned-leather rear seat, drove slowly past the teacher's house. A few minutes later, Thomas Farrell lowered himself from the car and walked, unaccompanied by his driver, to the front door.

Ronald answered the knock. He knew immediately who it was—even before he saw the car parked discreetly a short distance down the road. He stood in the doorway, momentarily unable to say anything.

"I take it that you're Ronald O'Carroll," said Thomas.

"I am indeed, sir."

"Then you will invite me in, if you don't mind."

Ronald stepped to one side. "Of course."

As he did so, he said to himself: *You are not to be intimidated by this man. You are the teacher. You are a graduate of the National University of Ireland. You are not some ignorant . . .*

They entered the living room. Thomas looked round it appraisingly. Then he turned to Ronald.

"They told me that your father was a very fine man," he said.

Ronald had not expected this.

"Thank you," he said. "He's retired now. He's living near Sligo."

Thomas nodded. "So I hear."

There was a silence.

"We have somebody working on the farm, you know, who was taught by him. A fellow by the name of Severin."

Ronald raised an eyebrow. "Yes . . ."

Thomas interrupted him. "They're not a good family," he said. "Some of them . . . Well, the least said about them the better. But this fellow—the fellow who works for me—is different. He says that your father got him to make something of his life. He's very grateful to him, you know."

Ronald's relief showed.

"You're pleased to hear that?" said Thomas.

"It's a good thing to hear that of one's da," said Ronald. "Who wouldn't be pleased?"

Thomas crossed to the mantelpiece, where there was a photograph of Ronald's parents. "He looks a lot like you," he said.

Ronald shrugged. "So people say."

Thomas turned to look at him directly. Ronald tried not to flinch at the intensity of the gaze.

"You've been seeing my daughter," he said.

Ronald took a deep breath. "We've been seeing one another, yes."

"Driving around in my car together," said Thomas.

"She invited me," said Ronald quietly.

Thomas suddenly took two steps forward, bringing himself right up against Ronald. He reached out to grip the lapels of the younger man's jacket. When he spoke, Ronald smelled something on his breath. It was not alcohol, but aniseed, he thought.

"She's hiding you from me, you know. She hasn't wanted me to know . . ." He broke off, releasing the lapels. "Kelly has told me. That's how I know. My own daughter won't speak about it."

Ronald plucked up his courage. "Perhaps she thinks you won't approve . . ."

This was brushed aside, but not in a tone of anger. "She's all I have, Mr. O'Carroll. She's everything to me."

Ronald did not reply. He was unsure what to say.

Thomas reached out to touch his sleeve. It was a curious gesture; one of supplication, it seemed. "So please don't take her away. Please don't take my whole life away from me."

Ronald gasped. "I hadn't intended . . ."

"Please marry her," said Thomas. "Please marry her and then come and live on the farm. Don't go off to Dublin like all the others. Everyone—going off to Dublin. We have two empty houses—fine buildings. I'd get one done up just for you." He paused. "And I'd consider myself honoured to have a man of your quality marrying my only daughter. I would be proud. If you are anything like your father, that is—which I believe to be the case."

Ronald sat down. "I hadn't thought . . ."

"You think she might not agree to marry you? But, my dear fellow, she's besotted with you. A father can tell."

Suddenly the mood changed, and it seemed to Ronald that Thomas felt the matter was settled. He watched him as he moved to the bookshelf and reached for one of the books. "William Butler Yeats . . . I've heard that he's your man. He's just the thing this country needs."

"You read him?" asked Ronald.

"Not exactly," said Thomas. "Not as such. But then there are an awful lot of people who do." He opened the book and flicked through the pages. "He has a way with words, this fellow. You can tell, can't you?"

Words. He thought of how he would have to work out what to say. He would ask her tomorrow.

And when he did, she said, "Yes, I would love to marry you, Ronald O'Carroll."

She was smiling at him. "It's strange how two tacks could change our lives, isn't it?"

He looked steadfastly ahead. "Yes, it is."

"Or were there more?" she asked, with a smile.

He Wanted to Believe in Tenderness

I

Two people—a young man and a young woman—were looking at a photograph. Two people of their own age looked back at them. The young man holding the photograph had just said something that had surprised the young woman.

"Really?" she said, looking up, and when he nodded, she continued, "Where did you read about that?"

"Oh, somewhere—I forget. It was an article about *mateship*, of all things—the idea of a . . . well, a sense of fellowship. It's a particular thing we have in Australia. Or the word is, at least."

She smiled. She was a New Zealander; it was different, even if the outside world knew little of the distinction. "Just a man's thing."

"Women go in for it too, I suppose. They call it sisterhood."

He studied the photograph again.

"My grandfather," he said.

She leaned over and touched his brow lightly. "I love you so much," she said. "I don't know why, but I do."

He took her hand and pressed it briefly to his lips. He liked her *non sequiturs*. He said, "The Australian officers, you see, were closer to their men than the British were. There wasn't a sense of distance between them. That had an effect, you know, on morale and, well, on physical well-being too. They looked out for them more. They helped them survive."

"Survive those terrible things they say the Japanese did?"

"Oh, they did them all right. Yes. When all that was going on."

He looked at the photograph. The afternoon sun was still warm on his face as it was in the picture, on the face of his grandfather who, when the photograph was taken, was about to leave Melbourne, on the first stage of his journey to Malaya.

She said, "I find pictures of smiling soldiers just so sad. So sad. How could they have smiled? How could *anyone* have smiled?"

"They did," he said, and then added, "But have you noticed that women who are photographed with them—their girlfriends, their wives—are smiling in a different way? Have you noticed that?"

She frowned. "Maybe. Why?"

"Is it because women *know?*" he asked.

She did not answer. He was right, though; she had always thought that women somehow knew more about how the world was, even if they were prevented from using that knowledge to full effect—prevented by men, who wanted to hold on to the privileges they had. That was going to change, and was already changing. Yet she did not want to *destroy* men; she did not want men to become discouraged, to give up, to stop being men. She wanted men to be strong. She wanted maleness to survive the loss of power.

But then her mind returned to the photograph. She turned to him and said, "You know the really interesting thing about these old photographs?"

"How they took them?"

"No . . . well, that's interesting enough, I suppose—in its way. But what really fascinates me is the question of how people got to where they are at the moment the photograph is taken. Who are they? How did they come to be where they are?"

"I told you: that's my grandfather."

"Yes, but how did he get to be *there*—that exact place—wherever it is."

He shrugged. "This was taken in Melbourne."

"So . . . how did he get to be there? How did he get to be in Australia in the first place? Where did they—you, for that matter—all come from?"

"Everyone comes from somewhere," he said. "Didn't we all migrate from Africa, originally? Even the aboriginal peoples?"

He made a gesture that seemed to suggest that the question was an impossibly complicated one.

"Yes," she said. "I suppose so. And we're all cousins, aren't we? Very, very distantly, I mean."

He thought about this. She was right: everybody came from somewhere else or owed his or her presence to somebody who had made the decision to travel from a long way away. Newcomers, he thought, even if after three, four generations; and if people claimed otherwise, they were just trying to justify excluding those who had arrived more recently, or who would like to arrive, given the chance.

"It makes one want to weep," he said.

"What makes one want to weep?"

"History," he replied.

2

The man in the photograph, sitting on the deck of a boat with a young woman at his side, was called David, and he was an only child. His father, Lou Rowse, owned a small agricultural machinery business in Bendigo. Lou was a Cornishman who had gone out to Australia in 1907 to join a childless uncle who had offered him a job and a chance to escape the poverty of life in England. "It's the richest, most powerful country there is," his Uncle Jack wrote to him, "and yet what do the likes of you have? England owns the world—look at the red on the map—and yet it can't give her people a proper breakfast. Why? Because the working man can't get a decent chance."

The mention of breakfasts was an odd way of putting it, but the words had struck a chord in the mind of the young Cornishman. A decent breakfast. It was true: sometimes he got a piece of bacon or a sausage for his breakfast, but this did not happen every day; most days it was bread, with a thin spreading of lard—a *sniff of lard,* as his mother put it. This would be accompanied by a thin porridge and some milk, or curds of milk. And here was his Uncle Jack, a miner and prospector, talking about Australia and the lavish breakfasts they had there; not that he gave details, so it was left to him to imagine the plates of fried mushrooms, the abundant rashers of bacon, the generous slices of toast covered with real butter, yellow and creamy, on which thick-cut marmalade had been spread. That was a breakfast to set you up for the day, and that, in essence, was what his Uncle Jack was offering.

Uncle Jack had never found gold, but Lou was told that he would. "You find gold if you look hard enough," said his father. "He'll find it all right, if I know Jack."

He was sent the fare for his passage, along with six pounds. He used two of these pounds to buy a suit, and ten shillings to buy a large trunk and a pair of best boots. He was wearing these boots, the leather still stiff and shiny, when he arrived in Melbourne. His uncle met him at the docks. "You're a strapping boy," he said admiringly. "Sixteen, now?"

"Sixteen, sir."

"No, none of that. I'm your Uncle Jack, right? We don't go in for none of that out here. One man's as good as the next." He put an arm about the boy's shoulder. "You're going to do fine out here. Look after yourself, you see—that's the ticket."

They travelled to Bendigo by train, the line winding

through a landscape that Lou found familiar and unfamiliar at the same time. There were the things one would recognise anywhere—roads, houses, churches; there were hills and farms and sheep; but there was something that was unlike anything he had seen before—a sky so high and wide and empty that he felt dizzy just squinting up at it from the window of the railway carriage. There were trees that were quite different from the trees he was familiar with—the oaks and hawthorns of his boyhood.

Jack was proud of Bendigo. "You see all this," he said, pointing to the street outside the railway station. "All built on gold." He paused. "Wait till you see our town hall. And our trams too. Big fountains too—we've got a place called Pall Mall—anything they have in London, we have here. Anything."

"Where's your mine?" asked Lou.

Jack sniffed. "Not my own mine, actually. There's one I lend a hand with. I never found anything myself, although I'm still looking, you know."

They made their way to Jack's house. "Nothing fancy," he said. "But it's got a roof and four walls. What more does a fellow need?"

The plot was a dusty half-acre. There had been attempts

to grow shrubs of some sort, but these had been abandoned, leaving small areas of dejected wilderness. Along one side of the plot was a line of eucalyptus trees, casting a shadow that gave protection, in that direction at least, from the sun. That night Lou heard the wind moving the branches of the trees. It made a sound like the sea, he thought, and for a moment he was back on that long sea journey that took him from everything he had known to put him here, in this strange land, friendless and alone, apart from an uncle he had never met before.

3

Jack introduced Lou to a man who said he would give him a job.

"He sells rope," Jack said. "Rope's the thing of the future, now that gold isn't doing too well. Rope's different. You don't have to dig for it, and they're going to need a lot of rope."

He liked the smell of rope, and its texture too. This enthusiasm made him a good salesman: if you believe strongly enough in something, then you can persuade others to believe in it too. He was promoted and his salary, meagre at first, was almost doubled. Now he was able to afford to rent a room rather than to live in the lean-to extension to his uncle's house.

He was worried that his uncle might resent his departure, but that did not happen.

"No offence taken," said Jack. "A man's got to stand on his own two feet."

He found lodging closer to the centre of town, in the house of a gold prospector's widow. There he had the breakfasts he had dreamed about.

"This," he said, pointing to his plate, "is the reason I came to Australia."

"As good a reason as any," she said.

Four years after Lou's arrival, Uncle Jack disappeared. He left a note on the kitchen table, and Lou found that when he went to look for him.

"I tried," the note said, and not much else. There was no forwarding address nor any indication where he was going.

"People go walkabout," said the widow. "And I hear he had debts. A lot of the prospectors do. The suppliers get paid if they find gold, but not if they don't." She shrugged. "Business."

"He could at least have said goodbye," said Lou.

"Then his creditors would have been able to get at you," said the widow. "This way, you don't know anything. What you don't know, you can't tell."

He continued to work with rope until he met a man in the bar of the hotel who said that agricultural machinery was the business to be in. "Farmers need these things," he said. "Tractors, ploughs, harvesters." Each was given the weight of a word in a litany. "Carts. Winnowers. Wire cutters."

Lou was convinced, and agreed to put what savings he had into a new venture. It was a success, although the partner—the man he had met in the bar—turned out to be a bigamist and left hurriedly for Adelaide. Lou now owned the entire business, which was growing rapidly. Jack had been right: people needed rope.

He met Dolly Lancaster, the receptionist in the Grand Hotel, at a party to celebrate his twenty-sixth birthday, and married her six months later. David was born two years after that, just when they were beginning to wonder whether Dolly would have trouble conceiving.

He was a particularly precious child to them, as the doctor had warned her she could have no more. She watched him in his cradle at night, sitting silently beside him until she herself dropped off to sleep. Sometimes Lou found Dolly still there in the morning, having not moved from her vigil.

"Don't wrap him up in cotton wool," he warned. "Boys learn by scraping their knees."

She knew that he was right, but could not help herself. "When something is as precious as that, it's really hard to let go, Lou. It just is."

He understood. "I have three precious things in my life," he said to Dolly. "You, my boy, and the business. Three things."

"You deserve it," said Dolly. "The moment I saw you in the hotel—the very first time—I knew that you were a kind man. I knew that you were going to ask me to marry you."

Lou laughed. "Get away!"

"No, I did—I swear it. I thought: *That's a good man and he's going to be my husband.*"

"I love you so much," he said.

She took his hand, and kissed him.

Several times a day they exchanged kisses. David watched them, bemused by the ways of the adult world. He kissed the dog, a Sydney terrier called Bob. "We don't kiss dogs," said Dolly. "Not in this family. It's unhygienic."

"He likes it," said David.

"That may be, but you don't want to get dog germs," she said.

"Don't kiss the dog," said Lou sternly. "You hear me? Don't kiss the dog."

David was loyal, and saw in the dog a quality of loyalty that seemed missing in the human world. "Dogs are good," he wrote in a school essay. "They don't drop you for other friends, they don't mind what you're like, a dog will never let you down."

The teacher wrote in the margins of his exercise book: "This is a very good essay, David. You are right about dogs. They are very loyal creatures. Remember, though, that each sentence must end with a full stop—a comma will not do. A comma is just like taking a breath. And it's *their* not *there* when you're talking about what people possess."

4

His strongest memory of childhood was of waiting for the beginning of the school holidays. That came achingly slowly, but when the day arrived the whole school was gripped with an electric excitement. The holidays themselves seemed endless, particularly in the first days—a blissful period during which he would spend hours with his friends at their favourite dam, fishing for the giant whiskered barbel that were rumoured to live there but that had never been seen, making camp fires on which they cooked roo steaks, riding their bicycles along the town's perimeter roads until heat and thirst drove them indoors.

He was aware that his father drank too much and that his drink problem was becoming steadily worse. He picked this up from his mother's look when his father returned from work each evening and immediately poured himself a whisky. He listened to their arguments: "Not too much, Lou. You know how strong that stuff is."

"Doll, I've been drinking since I was knee high to a grass-hopper. I know my limits."

"Too much is bad for the liver."

"My liver is used to it."

"You know what Dr. Bamfield says. He said the fact that you're alive is something of a minor miracle."

"The fact that *any* of us is alive is a minor miracle," he retorted.

He worried for his father. On one occasion, when he was ten, he accompanied him to an agricultural show. On the journey home, his father drove back by an unusual route, stopping outside a house in an unfamiliar part of town. "Wait in the car," he said. "I won't be long."

He watched his father go inside. It was dusk, and a light was switched on in one of the front rooms. A blind was pulled down at the window.

He entertained himself by counting the stars as they appeared in the sky. Then, bored with this, he let himself out of the car and went to sit by a small pond that had been created in the garden of the house. There were tadpoles in the water.

He looked up. His father was emerging from the front door. He glanced briefly over his shoulder, and then leaned towards the woman who was showing him out. He heard the sound of voices—his father's voice, and then hers. He heard laughter.

He ran back to the car, shielded from view by a hedge of stunted willow. They had learned a song at school: *I shall hang my harp on the weeping willow tree, and never more will think of thee . . .*

His father returned to the car. There was whisky on his breath; David could always tell.

"Good boy," said his father. "Just doing some business."

"Are they buying a tractor?" he asked.

His father glanced at him. "Maybe."

He knew this was not true, and he was shocked that his father should lie to him.

"Don't tell your ma we stopped by here," he said, as they drove off. "I don't want her to think I spend all my time working. Understand?"

He nodded.

His father gave him a peppermint. "Would you like two bob?" he asked.

He said he would; he thought it was a lot of money.

"Fair enough," said his father. "I'll give you two shillings when we get back."

David knew that something was being purchased, but he was not sure what it was.

Relations between his parents became increasingly tense. Kissing had stopped long ago, and now there were long periods of silence, punctuated with sighs from Lou. David watched, but could not find the words he felt he should say. He wanted them to be friends; he wanted them to stop the arguments he could not help but overhear after he went to bed and they thought he was safely asleep.

Then he heard the last of these exchanges. It was on a Sunday night, and his mother had been listening to a serial on the radio. His father had been out, but came back after David went to bed.

He heard him come in. He heard a bath being run.

"What do you want that for? You normally bathe in the morning. Why the bath now?"

His father's voice was slurred. "Cleanliness is next to godliness. Ever heard that, Dolly?"

"You've been with that woman. That's why."

There was a brief silence. Then: "So?"

"Don't you care any more? Don't you care any more about your son?"

"Of course I care." And then there was a new note of defiance. "I'm leaving. Tomorrow."

"Going where? To her?"

"She has a place up in Queensland. I'm going there. Sorry, but I can't see any other way."

"Then go. Just go. Go and drink yourself to death with this floozy of yours. Good riddance." There was a pause, during which he could not make out what they said. Then she spoke again, her voice rising with emotion. "I can't stand any more of this—Davey and I will be better off without you. Just get out."

The bathroom door slammed.

He lay quite still. He thought that he might go and plead with his father; surely if he begged him he would stay. But would his mother want that? He remembered what she had said: it would be better for everybody if he went.

In the morning, he woke up to find his father standing by his bed, wearing his coat and a pastoralist's hat. There was a lengthy and not very coherent explanation. "Your ma and I have been having our little differences, see, and sometimes when it's like that, it's best to go your separate ways."

He closed his eyes, willing this not to be happening. It was what you did as a child: you willed away those things you did not want to be. Sometimes it worked; but not now.

"You understand that, don't you? It doesn't mean that I don't love you as much as I always have—I do, of course—but I'm going to go and live up in Queensland for a while and see how things work out up there. I've got that fellow, Hopkins, to run the business for me—that'll give you and your ma all the money you'll need. You won't want for anything."

He lay immobile. How was it possible for a man to leave

his own family? How could such a thing come about? How could his father understand so little about loyalty?

At last he spoke. "Can I see you?"

The question seemed to please his father. "Of course you can see me," he replied. "You can come up north any time—in the school holidays. I'll have a cattle station up there, you know, Davey—I'm going with a friend, you see, and she's been left a half interest in one by her grandfather. That's great, isn't it? Half a station! Me!"

"I wish you'd stay," he whispered.

"What's that you say?"

"Nothing."

His father bent down to kiss him on the forehead. "Be good, son. Work hard at school. Show them what you can do." There was a pause. "Look after your ma, too. Get that? Look after Ma."

David started to sob, but his father neither saw nor heard this, as he had straightened up and was walking across the room. He turned at the door, raised a hand to wave, and then left. A few minutes later his mother came in and held him tightly to her as he sat up in bed. She dried the tears from his cheeks. She said, "We'll be all right, Davey. Just you and me—we'll be all right."

5

Lou left the family in 1931, when David was twelve. They heard from him every three months for the following two years, and then the letters—all of them formal and giving very little personal news—stopped coming. David received birthday cards and money was wired at Christmas, but his father ceased to play much of a part in their lives.

Dolly proved resilient, and was, as she had suspected, better off without Lou. She met a man whom she started to see—a teacher from the local senior school, whose passion was woodwork. He did not move in, but he was often about the place and appreciated by David, to whom he taught carpentry skills.

Dolly forgave Lou, and even started talking fondly about him. David did not. "He was disloyal," he said. "He was disloyal to you, Ma. How can I forgive that?"

"You can forgive most things," she said. "And if we don't forgive people, then how do we get on with life? You'll always be thinking of things that happened a long time ago. How can you get on with life if your mind is full of old stuff?"

"I don't want to forgive him. Ever."

"Well, it's up to you. But remember: he's your father, and you only get one father in this life. Just one."

At eighteen he went to university in Melbourne to study mechanical engineering. He had shown an aptitude for tinkering with machinery, and with his strong school record the university was keen to enrol him. Boarding was arranged for him with a family who were distantly related to his mother. They lived in North Fitzroy, and he travelled to lectures each day by tram.

At the beginning of his third year at university, war broke out in Europe. Events at that distance seemed very remote: he was not quite sure where Poland was, and looked closely at the map printed on the front page of *The Age*. But in spite of this remoteness, few questioned that this was their battle too. The Empire stood or fell with the mother country; everybody understood that very well. And it was the Empire that protected them from the threat from the East, and from the posturing of Japan.

He joined up at twenty-one, before he finished his degree. The university promised him that his place would be open when he came back. "It won't last long," his professor assured him. "Six months, I'd say."

"Could be longer," he said.

The professor was not convinced. "Could be. But look at the facts; look at the countries lined up against Hitler and his blackshirt windbags. You've got France—they're on our side. Massive army, I understand. Canada—big country. Then there's the rest of the Empire. South Africa and so on. India, too. Look at the Indian Army—countless men ready to serve; countless. Gurkhas, too, from Nepal. And it's just the Germans, with very few friends. They're outnumbered, David. No doubt about it, in my view."

He was sent to a barracks for his initial training and was then allocated to a transport unit. After three months he was given two weeks' leave and he returned to Bendigo. At a party at the house of a school friend, he met a girl called Hannah. She was Jewish.

He fell in love with her, and invited her to the town's cinema—the local way of making a declaration. They held hands. The following day he took her to dinner at the hotel. He said, "I'm sorry that I'm going away just as I've met you."

She looked at him. "We can see one another when you come back," she said. "I'll wait."

"Do you really mean that?"

"Yes, I do. I'll wait." She gave no thought to what she was saying. It was as if the lines had been scripted for her; that was what women said to men about to go off: *I'll wait.*

He drove her back to her house, but she asked him not to come in. "It's nothing personal," she said. "But my father . . ."

"Yes?"

"My father might not be pleased about this."

"About us?"

She nodded. "He's Jewish, you see. We're all Jewish. He won't want me to . . . to be seeing a boy who isn't Jewish." She looked at him despairingly. "Can you understand that?"

"Yes, but . . ."

"It's not the way I feel. I don't care what people are. Do you?"

He smiled. "Fathers often don't approve of their daughters' boyfriends. There's nothing new in that."

"It's a big thing in Jewish families. They don't like people to . . . to go outside, so to speak." She hesitated. "One of my cousins did. She married a boy she met in Sydney. My uncle wouldn't go to the wedding. My father said to me, 'Never do to us what Rebecca did.' He said that."

He shook his head. "What difference does it make?"

"A lot." But then she added, "To some people. Not to me. I think I should be able to see whoever I want to see." She relished the idea of standing up to her father, who had always expected the family to agree with him on every matter. He spoke as if he had the authority of the prophets behind him, but she would submit no longer. She did not care what he called her; the important thing for her was that she would lead her own life, according to her own lights, and with no interference from him. He did not know the answer to everything, as he liked to pretend. His was not the only way of looking at things; there were other people too.

"So do I."

He was puzzled. It had happened so quickly; he had not imagined that falling in love would be such a sudden and conclusive business, as the songs said it would be. He had mocked all that, thinking that it would never happen to him; but now he realised that what everybody said was true. He had not imagined that another person could so completely captivate you, could seem so inevitable.

Just before he had to report back to the barracks, he said to her, "I meant what I said. Everything."

She said, "And so did I. I don't want you to go. I can't bear the thought of you in the army. Going somewhere far away."

He tried to smile. "The army is fine. You spend all your time doing drill and waiting for things to happen. And then nothing happens and you go back to doing drill. That's the army for you." He paused. "I don't think I'm going anywhere."

"But still . . ."

"No, I'm telling you: the last thing the army wants to do is to actually do anything."

"Then what about the Germans?"

He thought about this. "The Germans will give up. They can't win."

His confidence was infectious. "Good," she said. "How hateful they are."

"The British will wipe the floor with them," he said. "The French too. Watch it happen."

6

When he was sent abroad, it was to Malaya, where he became part of a small Australian unit sent to boost the strength of a Scottish infantry regiment. The Scots had been short of transport, and David's unit had been detailed to help them.

He wrote to Hannah from the small coastal town they were defending. "When you get this will be anybody's guess. Maybe we will have moved on from here by the time this arrives—maybe not." He was not allowed to give the location, nor many other details, but he was able to write about the boredom of military life. "Nothing happens," he said. "We are in charge of the vehicles and we service them, as best we can, and carry out repairs. But we don't really go anywhere, and nothing ever seems to happen. The locals are friendly enough and sell us fresh vegetables and whatever else we need. They don't seem to be worried, although the planters are pretty anxious about the Japanese. They say they could invade at any moment and they're not sure whether our defences are up to dealing with an invasion. Many of them have sent their wives and children back to Kuala Lumpur or Singapore—others seem to think there's no chance of anything happening here. I've joined the library at the planters' club, and we're allowed to take out three books at a time. I've just finished a book by Trollope and some short stories by Somerset Maugham. A lot of the people in the club have strong views on Maugham, you know: they say that he accepted the hospitality of people out here and then wrote scathingly about them in his stories. I can't tell:

some of the characters in the stories I read seemed rather like some of the people I've met, but I think that's inevitable. After all, there are only a limited number of types, don't you think? Sooner or later a fictional character is going to match somebody or other, even if the author's never met the person in question. You can't blame Somerset Maugham for writing about what he saw, can you?"

She wrote back: "I wish you were coming back soon. Life in Bendigo is *very* dull, although last week there was a burglary at Mrs. Thompson's house and she went and died of shock. Apparently that can happen—you can die of shock. There was something on the ABC about that. They interviewed a doctor who said that being frightened to death was a real possibility. I don't know, but I was interested to hear it."

He kept her letters in a small box. This he tucked into his kit bag, alongside his shaving kit and the diary in which he made an entry every Friday. He was lonely in the army. He had been made an officer, but there were no other Australian officers in the town. The Scottish officers were courteous, but seemed reserved. He found them distant in their manner; not snobbish—just distant, with that diffidence that he had heard was so common among the Scots.

One evening an aeroplane came out of the sky and flew past their defences at a low height. He was standing outside one of the trading stores, and stepped out into the road to wave to the pilot. He assumed that the plane was British, and he wondered why it should have such an unusual shape and make a sound unlike any British plane.

He waved to the pilot when he was still some way away, and it seemed to him that his wave was acknowledged by a movement of the plane's wings. But then, with a noise that sounded like an angry cough, a splatter of rounds from the aircraft's guns traced a pattern of small eruptions across the tarred surface of the road. There was a further burst of fire, and this was followed by a screaming, shrill and persistent.

He felt a sudden sense of outrage. The plane was Japanese and it had just fired bullets into a busy street. The pilot must have seen that there were people around—how dare he set out to kill people like that? What was he thinking of?

The screaming intensified. People were running, and he heard nearby the shrill note of a siren. There was a small knot of people on the other side of the street on which he was standing. There was wailing now, and he saw a woman supporting a man who had blood streaming from his head.

It was the first casualty of war that he had seen, and he felt a sudden, raw shock. He was in a war—not in some strange bureaucratic drama of drill and boredom, but in a matter of blasted flesh and terror.

He returned to scenes of confusion at company headquarters. One of the Scottish officers told him that they had been ordered down to Singapore, to help shore up the defences of the island. "They thought the Japs would try it on from the sea," said this officer. "But now it looks as if they're going to do it by land."

He organised such transport as he could muster. Civilian cars were requisitioned and marshalled into a rag-bag convoy. Others joined, including a group of American missionaries and their converts. "We must get these good people to safety," said one of the missionaries. "We cannot leave them to the mercies of the Japanese."

A woman—one of the converts—gave birth on the journey south. They stopped the missionaries' car and moved her into a truck occupied by a group of Scottish soldiers. The baby, when it arrived, was wrapped in a kilt provided by one of the men.

One of the men for whom he was responsible—a man

who had been a fireman on the Ghan train—told him what he had heard about the Japanese in Korea. "My mate," he said, "saw a Japanese officer chop off a traffic policeman's head—in the street. It was right in front of him. My mate was in a rickshaw, and the rickshaw bloke just leapt off his bike and ran away. The Korean's head came right off."

He looked out of the window at the impenetrable green wall of jungle. He wanted to believe in tenderness; he wanted to believe in kindness, but now, perhaps, it was too late. Something had been unleashed that would make it impossible to go back to what had been before.

And then it all happened very quickly. His unit was one of the last to cross the causeway into Singapore. They were uncertain whether they should mine the road behind them: there was an order, and then there was a countermanding order—somebody else would do it; there were still people to come. Eventually they pressed on into a place where panic and torpor seemed to hold equal court. He came across a young boy sitting on a suitcase, reading a book about butterflies, who looked up at him and asked him whether he knew when his father would be coming to collect him. On a veranda behind the building his company had occupied—

a trading warehouse, half-filled with bales of printed cotton—he stumbled over a group of elderly Chinese men playing Mah Jong. They did not look up from their clicking tiles and ignored him, as interlopers had been ignored for centuries in their world.

The surrender came when he was struggling with a buckled leg on his camp bed, trying to make it fold correctly. He heard a single shot, followed by shouting. There was the sound of a vehicle revving its engine and after that a brief silence. Then barked commands in Japanese.

7

This doctor, at least, seemed to have the time to talk to him.

David fingered the button of his jacket. The sunlight made his eyes hurt for some reason, although they had told him this would get better. "You're a psychiatrist, aren't you?"

The doctor smiled. "Well, I do a lot of work at the mental hospital. I've had a bit of training in that sort of thing. But I do other things too. You have to, when you're in the army." He paused. "Actually, I'd like to be an ear, nose, and throat surgeon. That's what I'd really like, but the army doesn't let you do everything you want to do. You must have noticed that."

He responded to the joke. "A bit."

The doctor looked out of the window. "Now that the war's over, I'm hoping to get out. I've had an offer of a job over in Perth that I'm keen to take up. But they won't let me go—not just yet. I suppose it's you chaps . . ."

"Sorry to keep you, Doc."

"Not your fault." He pointed up at the ceiling; at higher authority.

"I don't think there's anything wrong with me, you see."

The doctor played briefly with a pencil on his desk. "No? Well, I suspect you're right. But we have to be careful, you know. We can fix a man's body, but sometimes there are other things that can cause trouble a bit later on. The body and mind, you see, are pretty much interconnected."

"I'll be happy once I can't see my ribs any more."

The doctor laughed. "Yes. And according to this . . ." He took a piece of paper out of a file. "According to this, you're putting on weight all right—it's just a bit slow. They were wondering whether there might be something else going on—something holding back the physical recovery."

The doctor looked at him enquiringly. David shrugged, but his shoulders hurt as he did so; it was the bone against the skin, because there was so little flesh left.

"A lot of men," said the doctor, "have come back full of . . . well, I happen to think the only word for it is sorrow. I know that's not a medical term. You won't find it in the textbooks. But . . ." He did not finish the sentence.

David looked at him. Sorrow?

"Sorrow over what they've been through," continued the doctor. "Sorrow at what they've seen." He paused. "I've heard just about everything, you know. I've had men sitting where you are, breaking down, crying like children, sobbing their hearts out over what happened to them. Ghastly things. Things that just leave one simply confounded over the capacity of people to cause pain to others."

Their eyes met.

"You know what I'm talking about," said the doctor. "You don't have to tell me—unless you want to. It helps some people to talk, but not all. I think it depends on the individual."

"Sorrow," said David quietly.

"Yes? You feel it?"

"I suppose I do."

The doctor picked up his pencil again, playing with it, tapping it lightly against the desk. "Where? Where do you feel that sorrow? Where does it come from?"

David closed his eyes. He could see one face in particular; one uniform. He heard screams. He felt the sun beating down on him and the thirst that brought—the unremitting, unquenchable thirst.

"You know something?" he said to the doctor. "Goats and chickens."

"Goats and chickens?"

"There were ten of us in this room, you see. It used to be part of a school before they converted it into a pen for us. A tiny room, with not enough space for all of us to lie down at once. So we had to take it in turns. But there was something about this room that we liked very much, and that was that it was half basement and half ordinary room. And there was a window—a barred window—that looked out at ground level on to a yard in which chickens would poke around. Japanese chickens. And the occasional goat."

The doctor was watching him.

"The bars were quite wide apart—not wide apart enough for a man to crawl out, but quite wide enough for a chicken—or a goat—to be grabbed and then pulled through. We saved grains of rice and reached out of the window to put them on the ground outside. This attracted chickens and then one of us, a chap called Tommy Sprigge, reached out and caught a chicken by the neck and dragged it through the bars. Same thing for the goats, as long as they weren't too big. Kids were fine—mature goats were a bit more difficult.

"And then in five minutes—not a second more—the chicken would be dispatched and plucked, ready for cooking. Same thing for the goat. Bang. End of goat."

The doctor's eyes widened.

"We also ate rats. Sprigge's arm would shoot out—like a snake striking—and grab the rat. They squealed, and often bit him, but he just laughed it off."

"I see," said the doctor.

"Because the world is full of pain," said David. "Pain and terror and hunger and . . . I'm not sure if I've left anything out."

"I think you've described the human condition rather well," said the doctor. "Is that where your sorrow comes from?"

"Yes," he said.

The doctor became businesslike. "You have a girlfriend, I understand."

"Well, she's a girl I met."

The doctor referred to his notes. "I'm told that she's been in touch, trying to get to see you. I gather that you've refused."

He was silent for a while. Then he said, "I can't let her see me like this."

The doctor nodded. "I can understand how . . ."

"How ashamed I feel," David said.

"Yes. I wouldn't try to deny shame. We all feel shame."

"Well, it's what I feel when I go anywhere near a mirror."

The doctor folded a piece of paper he had extracted from the file. "But you will see her eventually? When you've recovered condition?"

He looked down at his hands. They were shaking.

"You see," said the doctor, "the human body knows sorrow when it encounters it. And the only way to deal with that is to look at the sorrow—look it in the eye—and face it down."

He kept his eyes downcast. "Maybe," he said.

"No," said the doctor. "Definitely." He waited for a few moments before continuing. "That's a strange thing to remember. Well, not strange, I suppose, but it's surprising that you should talk about that when I imagine you saw very shocking things—the cages, the beatings, the executions."

"Perhaps. But you see . . ."

He did not know how to continue. The doctor waited for a few minutes, but nothing came, and so he leaned forward and put a hand on David's shoulder. It was so thin—like touching bone, but he had seen so many men in that state. "Time," sighed the doctor. "Time heals, doesn't it?" He sighed again. "A rather defeatist thing for a doctor to say, I suppose."

"But true."

The doctor looked up sharply. "I think you're going to be all right," he said. "Most men say nothing if I go on about what time can do. Or they deny it. Or they simply cry."

"Your own job can't be all that easy, Doc. And who fixes you up when it all gets a bit too much?"

"Time," said the doctor.

They both laughed.

8

"My job," his mother said, "is to feed you up. Correct?"

"Well, I'm still having trouble with my stomach."

Dolly brushed this aside. "The doc told me about all

that," she said. "But he said the most important thing was good food."

"If that's what he said . . ."

She put a cushion behind his back, making sure he was comfortable. "It can't be very easy sitting down for long when you're all skin and bone."

"I'm used to it. I didn't know shoulder blades were the shape they are."

"Or knees," she said, looking down.

"We're all skeletons underneath, I suppose." He leaned back against the cushion gingerly. "I don't want to go out—you know that, don't you?"

She had received a letter from the hospital and it had made that clear. "Not even a few short . . ."

He cut her off. "No. Not yet. I don't want people to see me."

She bit her lip. "Don't try to argue with him," a friend had warned her. This friend was a nurse; she knew. "You think you can chivvy them along—you can't."

So she said nothing. But then he said, "A few weeks maybe. I'll look a bit better then."

"You can be proud of the way you look," she muttered under her breath.

"What?"

"The way you look is like having a medal," she said. "People understand."

"That's as may be, but I'm not going out."

"All right, all right."

She bullied him into eating the large meals she had prepared for him. One morning she said, "You know these big breakfasts I make for you? Well, it's reminded me of something your father used to say."

He was silent; he did not encourage her to talk about Lou. She sensed this, but persisted. "He said that it was the idea of having big breakfasts that made him want to come to Australia all those years ago. Can you imagine that? Bacon, sausages, fried eggs—a reason for starting a new life."

He smiled, in spite of himself. "I'm going to burst at this rate, Ma."

"You're a long way off that, but you're getting there, you know. Mutton for lunch. I've got a beaut of a joint from Mr. Wallace. He knew it was for you and so he didn't charge. People are kind, aren't they?"

He tackled his breakfast. He had never imagined in Changi that he would find eating a chore. He had never imagined that he would be revolted by cream—by the mere sight of it—and that he would struggle to swallow the over-rich puddings that his mother prepared for him: pears with cream, tapioca with cream, sponge cake doused in sherry and then topped with cream.

Of course it worked, and two months later the doctor said, "You're no longer crook, young man. Fit as a fiddle—or almost."

Leaving the house, the doctor said, "Get him out now, Mrs. Rowse. Get him outdoors. Get him back to work, if possible, or to the university or wherever. Don't let him sit here."

David overheard. He had dreaded this moment, but he felt too weak to resist. He knew that he looked better, but he wondered what Hannah would say when she saw him. She had spoken to his mother and said that she was looking forward to seeing him again. As a friend? he wondered. Probably. So many men had found out that the words *I'll wait* might be well intentioned, but rarely meant what they purported to say.

He was wrong. When he eventually said that she could come to the house, her emotions were close to the surface. She was reproachful. "Didn't you want to see me?"

"Yes, but I had to get better first."

"You were ill?"

"In a manner of speaking. It was very tough in the camp. I ended up . . . a bit of a skeleton."

She tried to smile. "That would have made no difference to me."

He shrugged. "What have you been doing?"

"I did a bookkeeping course in Melbourne. Then I came back. I found a job."

"I see."

She waited. She had noticed his fingers, and how thin they still were. Did it take longer to put weight on one's hands because the body somehow decided what was important and what was not? Nobody died of thin fingers, after all.

Suddenly she said: "I don't care."

"About what?"

"About doing things the right way round. I don't care if you aren't going to ask me to marry you—I'll do the asking myself."

9

He returned to Melbourne to finish his degree. Hannah came too, and it was in Melbourne that they married. Dolly came from Bendigo for the wedding, which was a quiet affair in a register office, unattended by Hannah's parents. "I cannot give my blessing to this marriage," said her father. "You will always be my daughter—always—but I cannot celebrate something that breaks my heart as this does."

After his graduation, they returned to Bendigo to live with Dolly, who had several spare bedrooms and a room they could use as their private living room. David applied for and was given a job in the transport department of the municipal council. This did not test his engineering skills, being more administrative than technical, but conditions were good and the pay would enable them to save for a deposit on their own house.

They bought that house two years later, shortly before the birth of their daughter, Rachel.

"I am very happy," David said one afternoon.

He had expected her to echo what he said, but she did not. He looked at her, and he knew immediately that something was wrong.

"Is everything all right?" he asked.

She nodded. "Of course."

"It's just that I thought you might be a bit more enthusiastic."

"I'm seeing somebody else," she said flatly. "I wish I could have told you earlier, but somehow I haven't found the words."

10

After the divorce, he looked around for a job elsewhere. He knew that this would mean that he would only rarely see Rachel, but he found it too painful to remain in Bendigo. He was not sure that he could live with the knowledge that he might meet her in the street with her new man, a timber merchant with large premises in the centre of town. It would be better, he thought, to go away.

He wrote to his friend, Ronnie, who lived in Adelaide. Ronnie had been in Changi with him and they had kept in touch. Ronnie wrote back: "There's lots of work over here. I know of a new bus company that's looking for somebody with a bit of knowledge of how transport works. It's a man called Harris. He was in Singapore too but got out to Sumatra just before it fell and was put in the bag there. He'll take you, I'm sure of it."

He made the journey and was interviewed by Harris, who told him three minutes into their conversation that the job was his. "Can you start next week?" he asked.

He hesitated, but agreed. Harris handed him a key. "Go and take a look at this place. It's near the river. I can let you have it at half rental, with an option to buy after two years. It would suit you if you decide to get married again—Ronnie told me about your bad luck. You deserve better after what you went through."

He had never blamed Hannah. "Sometimes a marriage doesn't work. It just doesn't work."

Harris did not doubt that. "But I'm talking about justice, mate. That's what I'm talking about."

He saw his daughter four times a year, always without seeing Hannah. From time to time Dolly brought her down to stay in Adelaide, and he would take a week's leave in order to be able to entertain her. He had done well in the bus company, and had been given a share in the company by Harris, who had developed an interest in property development and was content to let David run that side of the business. He was now reasonably well off, but had remained in the same house that he had occupied when he first went to Adelaide. He became secretary of a cricket club, and was popular, often being invited to dinners and parties. But he did not remarry.

In 1958, when he was thirty-nine, Hannah was badly injured in a road accident. At the end of seven weeks in hospital she was discharged, but had lost the use of her legs. She went home to the timber merchant, who stayed two months before leaving her.

David heard about all this from Dolly, who said she had never liked Hannah's new husband and she was not surprised. David wrote to Hannah and told her how sorry he was to hear what had happened. She replied, thanking him and saying that she was grateful that she had at least survived the accident. "Please come and see me if you are in Bendigo," she said.

He made the journey two weeks later. They sat on her veranda and drank tea.

"When are you going back to Adelaide?" she asked.

For a few minutes he did not reply. Then he said, "I want to stay to look after you. I'll move back here."

She stared at him.

"I can't leave you like this," he said.

She was struggling. "I get help," she said. "The nurse comes in."

He shook his head. "You would be miserable being left all by yourself while Rachel is at school."

She put down her teacup and then buried her head in her hands. Her frame was racked with sobs. He said, "Please don't cry."

"I don't deserve you," she said. It took her some time to get the words out.

He stayed with her for the rest of her life. She died in 1995, when she was seventy-six. He survived her by four years. Shortly before his death, he said, while sitting on his veranda in Bendigo, "My life, you know, has not amounted to very much. I have been lucky, though, to have had a place to be proud of—this town—a chance on one occasion to stand up for something worth standing up for—the Second World War—and a handful of people to love—my wife, my ma, my daughter. I'm not sure that any of us is entitled to much more than that."

He did not know it, but his grandson heard him talking to himself. The young man stood stock-still, the hairs on the back of his neck stiff. He did not declare his presence, but moved away, back into the house, where he thought of each word that had been said—each word.

ABOUT THE AUTHOR

Alexander McCall Smith is the author of the No. 1 Ladies' Detective Agency series, the Isabel Dalhousie series, the Portuguese Irregular Verbs series, and the 44 Scotland Street series. He is professor emeritus of medical law at the University of Edinburgh in Scotland and has served with many national and international organizations concerned with bioethics. He was born in what is now known as Zimbabwe and was a law professor at the University of Botswana. He lives in Scotland.

Anthea Farrell, County Sligo

Harry, Jenny and friends, Argyll